Tom Trueheart
and the Land of
Myths and Legends

OXFORD
UNIVERSITY PRESS

Great Clarendon Street, Oxford OX2 6DP

Oxford University Press is a department of the University of Oxford.
It furthers the University's objective of excellence in research, scholarship,
and education by publishing worldwide in

Oxford New York

Auckland Cape Town Dar es Salaam Hong Kong Karachi
Kuala Lumpur Madrid Melbourne Mexico City Nairobi
New Delhi Shanghai Taipei Toronto

With offices in

Argentina Austria Brazil Chile Czech Republic France Greece
Guatemala Hungary Italy Japan Poland Portugal Singapore
South Korea Switzerland Thailand Turkey Ukraine Vietnam

Oxford is a registered trade mark of Oxford University Press
in the UK and in certain other countries

British Library Cataloguing in Publication Data
Data available

ISBN: 978-0-19-275564-3

1 3 5 7 9 10 8 6 4 2

Printed in Great Britain

Paper used in the production of this book is a natural,
recyclable product made from wood grown in sustainable forests.
The manufacturing process conforms to the environmental
regulations of the country of origin.

www.tomtrueheart.com

Tom Trueheart
and the Land of
Myths and Legends

IAN BECK

OXFORD
UNIVERSITY PRESS

Part One
In A Cold Place

Chapter 1

Once upon a time . . .
Tom Trueheart opened his bedroom window. It was early on a summer morning and he had no wish to disturb the rest of his family. He hoped, in fact, that they were all still fast asleep. He climbed outside, then paused and balanced for a moment on the windowsill. He looked across at the surrounding forest. The sky had an almost golden glow in the east, and he could see a flock of distant circling birds.

'I hope you're coming this time, Jollity,' Tom said under his breath, and then he shimmied all the way down the drainpipe.

3

He cheerfully scuffed his leather breeches on the wall as he jumped lightly down into the garden. He went to the place under the old tree root where he had hidden all his adventurer's things the night before. He retrieved his packstaff, which he had already packed tight with useful things to eat, plus some candles and tinderbox, a compass, a little metal opener, and some money.

He picked up his quiver of arrows and his bow, and, of course, his special birthday sword too. The blade sparked and flared just a little, and reflected a flash of gold from the sky as he slipped the sword into the scabbard on his belt. He checked that he had his Story Bureau maps and the letter which Cicero, the wise old forest sprite who controlled sprite magic and made things happen in the Land of Stories, had left to encourage him on his journey. He was excited at the possibility of seeing his old friend Jollity again, but just a little worried too, about them sharing yet another, and possibly even more dangerous, adventure than their last. He also felt just a slight twinge of guilt at the thought of deliberately missing his brothers Jack, Jackson, Jake, Jacques, Jackie, and Jacquot's weddings. The big wedding was finally to happen (again) today.

He had at least been there for their first try at the big occasion, which had been so cruelly interrupted, and look at all that had happened after that. Well, he had done his best to be a pageboy for them. He had pleased his mother. He had suffered wearing the awful white velvet pageboy suit just that once. Now it was time for a big new secret adventure to begin. Time to be brave, to play the hero, to go on the really important quest: to find his father, Big Jack the Giant Killer, rescue him, and bring him home.

Tom stood in the middle of the bright garden and breathed in deeply. The air was cool with the scent of flowers, and there was a gentle breeze. A sudden sense of freedom and happiness swept over him. It was a fine golden summer morning, and he was about to begin a new adventure. He looked up at the weathervane. A big glossy black crow perched there looking down at him.

'Is that really you, Jollity?' Tom said.

The bird looked back at him, tilted its head on one side, and said, 'Caw.'

Tom looked at the bird, and the bird looked back at Tom with its beady eyes.

'Only teasing,' said the bird after a moment. 'Of *course* it's me, Tom.'

'About time too,' said Tom, in a mock angry voice.

The bird fluttered down and settled on his shoulder.

'Right,' said Tom. 'Now that's better, feels just right. Jollity sitting on my shoulder, instead of me sitting on Jollity's shoulder. Come on, we've got an important secret mission to carry out. We have to go to the harbour first, I think,' said Tom.

'Aye aye, captain,' said Jollity.

Tom's mother, the kindly Mrs Nell Trueheart, had been awake since first light. She nodded and smiled to herself as she tucked the kitchen curtain back into place after watching Tom and Jollity walk away. 'That's my good boy,' she said proudly to herself. Then she had a sudden thought: it was an image of Tom walking back up that same path with his father, Big Jack, and both had their packstaffs jauntily over one shoulder. She shook her head and went and called up the stairs, 'Come on, now then, you lot, shake a leg, it's breakfast time, and it's your wedding day, all over *again*, in case you didn't know it, so look lively.'

Chapter 2

BESIDE THE SEA

6.33 P.M.

It was early evening by the time Tom and Jollity reached the coast. All the way, walking through the summer day, Tom had been worried about how he was actually going to find his father again and rescue him. He had had a secret meeting with Cicero who advised him to simply go to the harbour and charter a vessel. A sea fret had risen up and drifted across the little harbour town. It looked faded and almost ghostly. They headed, as advised by Cicero, to an old seafarers' tavern on the waterfront.

The inn sign creaked on its salt-rusted hinges as it swung lightly back and forth in the wind. The words,

Olde Admiral Benbow Inne, were painted in big letters on the sign under the portrait of an old sea captain. The sign had been worn and faded by years of sunlight and salt air. The creaking sound, the general evening gloom, and the air of misty desolation in this, the rougher end of the harbour town, made Tom shiver a little and draw his cloak tighter about his neck.

'That's the place,' Tom said, 'that's where Cicero said we should go.' The crow flew up and settled high on the iron sign support and scanned the harbour.

There were boats, and skiffs, and clippers of all descriptions. There were fully rigged pirate ships, rowing boats, and steam yachts. They all looked ready for any kind of story or adventure. Jollity flew back and landed on Tom's shoulder.

'There,' he said, 'if I sit on your shoulder again you'll look more like a pirate, and you'll need to do that to blend in once you are in there.'

'Right,' said Tom. 'Ready, Jollity, here we go then.'

He pushed open the inn door. The hinges squealed and squeaked, and a few heads turned to look at the new arrivals. Inside the inn it was warm and dark. The interior was lit by smoky coal fires, and a few sputtering oil lamps, and candles. It smelt of many things: of old beer, and wine, and rum; of exotic spices, salt water, and unwashed seafaring folk; and also very strong pipe tobacco.

'Ugh,' said Tom under his breath, 'it really stinks in here.'

He could just make out groups of figures in the dimness. They were either lined up at the bar or sitting around the small tables, scattered about the room. He could see the odd flash of a gold earring, the glint of a cutlass or two, or the dull shine of a dagger blade in the gloom. Jollity was right, this was a rough place, a pirate dive if ever there was one. Tom approached the bar, keeping his hand firmly on the hilt of his sword, and looking as tough as he could manage.

'What will it be then, my young shaver?' said the landlord, who wore an eye patch. He eyed up first Tom, and then Jollity the crow, with his one good eye. 'The children's menu for you, I should think,' he said. 'You get a lovely little "scary island" treasure map to colour in with these here wax crayons while you wait, too.'

Tom frowned and stared straight back at him.

'Nothing like that,' he said, and then lowering his voice, 'I am here to charter a vessel.'

'A vessel,' said the landlord with a note of surprise in his voice. 'Why you don't seem old enough to be but a cabin boy yourself. Chartering a vessel, now that costs money. It needs paying for, and the big question is, do you have it . . . the *money*, that is?'

At the word 'money' the low hum of muttered conversation in the room stopped, as if every ear had been tuned in to notice and respond on the instant to just that very word, money.

'We have a little money with us, and also we have things,' Tom replied a little too loudly.

The landlord shook his head. 'Things?'

'They are valuable things,' Tom whispered.

'I think you'd best talk to the gentleman over there. The one you will find warming his peg-leg in front of my fire, and all on one glass of rum a day, if you please. Mind what you tell him, though, he's a bit of a rogue,' said the landlord quietly, and winked his good eye.

Tom, with Jollity the crow still firmly, if nervously, on his shoulder, made his way over to the fireplace, where the tail end of a smoky fire was busily dying down. A large man sat in an old chair, with his wooden peg-leg stretched out in front of him. Like the landlord, he also wore an eye patch and like Tom he had a bird resting on his shoulder, but his bird was a brightly coloured parrot. The man looked up at Tom and his face cracked into a broad smile, showing a set of almost entirely gold teeth.

'Arrgh, what can I do fer ye, my lad,' he said in a very, very thick piratical voice.

'Excuse me, sir, but the landlord said I should speak to you about the possibility of chartering a vessel,' Tom said.

'A vessel, eh; is your name *Hawkins*, by any chance?'

'No, sir.'

'I was told to expect a Hawkins, first name Jim.'

'I am Tom Trueheart of the Adventuring Truehearts,' said Tom, 'and I need to charter a vessel for an adventure.'

'Oh, I'm the man for that, all right,' said the piratical man, and took a swig from his tankard. 'You look about the right age for young Hawkins; you sure you're not him?'

'Sure,' said Tom.

The pirate wiped his hand across his mouth. 'I'm not fussy, mind,' and he brought his face close to Tom's, 'provided, that is, you got the . . . *funds*.'

Tom shook his packstaff and there was the happy jingle of coins.

'Pieces of eight, pieces of eight,' cackled the parrot on the pirate's shoulder.

'Ssh, you,' said the pirate to the bird, which ruffled up its feathers, causing Jollity the crow to match it by ruffling his feathers too.

'Pay no mind to the bird,' said the pirate. 'Now coin is one thing but is there any sprite gold? Only I've been waiting a long time for my story to start, and waiting rum costs money see,' he whispered.

'Pieces of eight,' the parrot hissed.

The crow answered suddenly with a throaty 'Caw,' and both the birds ruffled up their feathers again and glared at one another with their beady eyes.

'What the bird is saying is that I am mostly interested in doubloons; doubloons of pure sprite gold,' said the pirate and again everyone in the inn fell silent around them.

'I don't think we have anything much at all in the way of sprite gold,' said Tom quietly.

The pirate took another swig from his tankard. 'For a proper scurvy crew like mine and a decent seaworthy vessel you'll need a quantity of that particular gold to smooth the way, lad, sorry,' and he shook his head.

'It's really a very important and secret adventure,' said Tom.

'No actual sprite gold, though, arrgh?' said the man with a hint of sympathy in his voice.

'No,' said Tom.

'Tell you what, lad, I've taken a liking to you, and my parrot likes the look of you and he likes the look of your fine bird there too. You seem like a brave young soul and I admire that.' He lowered his voice. 'We pirates have our own code of honour, whatever people say. Even though you're not this young Hawkins shaver that I'm meant to meet, I'm going to help you out. Somewhere in this hive of scum and villainy is the one they call,' and here he lowered his voice even further, to a whisper, 'the *Cat*.'

Both the birds fluffed their feathers again. The parrot raised its wings and Tom felt the crow's claws dig into his shoulder.

'The Cat,' Tom said.

'Ssh, aye, the Cat,' whispered the pirate. 'She has a small vessel, a one person crew, but tough and seaworthy as they come.' The pirate tapped his nose and winked his good eye.

'Where would I find this . . . Cat?' Tom asked.

14

'Why, back there in the snug bar,' said the pirate. 'But take care now how you go, and good luck, young lad. If ye should ever find yourself a nice hoard of sprite gold, come back to me and we'll do some proper business together, t'would be my pleasure.' The pirate raised his tankard.

'Pieces of eight,' the parrot squawked.

Chapter 3

A MEETING

7.24 P.M.

The snug bar in the back of the inn was even darker than the main bar. It was lit by just one smoky oil lamp which hung on a dusty chain over a large oval-shaped table. A group of characters were playing cards around the table in the gloom. Tom edged close to the table. He could see a hawk-nosed man in a full-bottomed wig of dark curls; he was holding his hand of cards in a metal arrangement attached to the hook where his hand would once have been.

'Make your bid, captain,' came a deep throaty purring sort of voice from the darkness. The man with the hook hand hesitated, looked at the cards, then looked up and saw Tom standing looking at him.

'Well,' he snapped in a very superior sort of voice, 'what do you think you are staring at, my little lost boy, eh? What's the matter, cat got your tongue, ha, ha?' The whole of the group around the table laughed.

'I'm not lost, sir,' said Tom nervously, 'I'm looking for the one they call the Cat.'

'Well,' came the smooth purring voice from the shadows once again, 'it looks like you've found her.'

It was then that Tom noticed that there was a girl sitting in the shadows at the other side of the table holding a hand of cards. She had hypnotically bright green eyes, which Tom noticed were staring straight at the crow perched on his shoulder.

'My, what a fine bird,' said the girl.

The crow ruffled its feathers and just said, 'Caw.'

Tom carried on. 'I was told you had a vessel,' he said. 'I need to charter a vessel for a really big adventure.'

'An *awfully* big adventure, don't you mean,' said the man with the hook, laughing knowingly and looking at Tom with a sneer on his face.

'Well, you are speaking to the right girl then, and no mistake,' the girl said, and put her hand of cards face down on the green-topped table. 'We can't do business in here; come with me.' The girl stood and the man with the hook quickly flipped her cards over.

'Knew you were bluffing,' he said and then raked some coins across the table with his hook.

The girl was taller than Tom. She led the way out of the dingy snug bar, through the back of the inn and out into a little cobbled yard. Oak casks and barrels were piled up against the wall, and there was a strong smell of rum.

'Now,' the Cat said, settling herself against one of the barrels, 'my vessel is small but very reliable. I can run on sail or steam, I crew myself, and she'll get you where you want to go. Which is where, by the way?' All the while she looked at Tom not unkindly with her big green eyes.

'We need to get over to the Land of Myths and Legends as soon as possible,' said Tom, and he pointed at the distant horizon far across the water.

The girl narrowed her eyes and let out a low whistle. 'I had a funny feeling you were going to say that. Surely

18

a dangerous place for a boy like you. The Land of Myths and Legends, a land way back in time. I admire your pluck. For a crossing like that I would need a special payment. What could you manage, then?'

Tom shook his packstaff and the coins jingled.

'Well, we have plenty of coins: some groats, some pennies, a shilling or two. Oh, and a note.'

'What value of note,' the Cat asked.

'A big five pound note, I think,' said Tom.

'Mmm, not bad; anything else?'

'One or two things of value, not very much really. Oh please, do help us, it is so important.'

'Show me,' said the Cat.

Tom untied his packstaff and laid the Trueheart cloth out on the top of a barrel lid. He poked around among all the things he had packed.

'Well, there's half a loaf of pumpernickel bread.'

'My, how you do tempt a girl so,' she said flashing her eyes at the crow, 'and?'

'Some nuts and raisins.'

'And?'

'A bottle of ginger beer.'

'And?'

19

'A cooked sausage.'

'And?'

'An apple.'

'And?'

'A piece of cheese.'

'Is that it?'

'Oh, and a jar of my mother's best home-grown honey made from her own bee hives,' Tom added.

'Honey, eh? Well now, that's better, I'm very, very partial to some sweet honey. I like the look of you, lad; I'm tempted to bother with you. Mmm,' she looked thoughtful for a moment, 'I must be mad but I'll take you.'

'Thank you, ma'am,' said Tom.

'My name's Tabitha,' the girl said extending her hand.

Tom took her hand and shook it. 'Tom Trueheart of the Adventuring Truehearts, and this is Jollity the crow.'

'Pleased to meet you,' Jollity said.

'Well, well,' said the girl. 'My, you didn't say he was a *talking* bird. Does he sing as well; I love to be sung to?'

'I've never heard him sing,' said Tom, 'but I'm sure he could if he wanted to.'

The crow ruffled his feathers and flew up and settled on a barrel far from the girl.

'When would you like to sail?' said Tabitha.

'Tonight, if possible,' said Tom.

'Come on then,' she said, 'we'd better go right away, no time to waste, the tide is up.'

Chapter 4

A CROSSING

A GENTLE BREEZE FROM THE

SOUTH-WEST, SEA CONDITIONS FINE.

8. 00 P.M.

Tabitha led the way along the quayside, past all the bobbing boats. She looked over her shoulder now and then, and smiled, showing her sharp white teeth.

'Play any instruments do you,' she asked, 'mandolin, concertina, that sort of thing?'

'No, miss, sorry,' said Tom.

'Pity,' she said, 'I like a song as I work.'

'I see,' said Tom, who thought that he had never met such a strange and interesting girl.

They were soon level with a neat little boat with a

22

furled mainsail, a tall brass chimney, and a warm light shining in the cabin.

'Welcome aboard,' Tabitha said, and led the way down the gangplank. They went into the cabin. A large friendly looking brown owl was sitting on the back of a chair. 'Oh, Owly, there you are,' she said. 'This elegant fowl is my first mate, my crew, my life, aren't you?'

'Tuwoo,' said the owl.

'We have crossed this stretch once or twice before doing little bits of secret business for sprites and so forth, but only up to a certain point at sea,' said the Cat. 'The trick is to avoid any monstrous entanglements.'

'Monstrous entanglements?' said Tom.

'Yes,' she said. 'There are monsters I'm afraid, mythical sea monsters, and plenty of them too, further on in near that boundary sea, just you wait.'

'Boundary sea?' said Tom.

'You don't know about that?' said Tabitha. 'That part of the sea marks a boundary between the time zones; once you cross it you go far back in history. I have never crossed it and I wouldn't.'

'I have to,' said Tom.

'You're a brave boy. Which section of the island are you heading for? It's a big place that divides north to south, as you can see here from this chart, straight across the middle?'

'That I don't know. What do you say, Crow?'

'I only flew near enough and high enough to identify just the island itself.'

'Well, straight from here as the crow flies, pardon the expression, would bring you to the North Lands or Norse Lands, the winter side. Further to the south is the summer side, the warm lands, the land with the "wine dark" sea.'

'We'll start at the Norse Lands,' said Tom, 'and then work our way south from there.'

'You are sure?' she asked.

Tom nodded.

'Come on, then,' she said, 'the moon is nearly up, no time like the present, as they say. And where you are going there really is no time like the present, as you'll discover. I'll just cast off.'

She bustled about below and on the deck, and consulted the charts and maps in the cabin. The little motor soon sputtered into life and they set off at a steady pace, the engine making a pleasant chugging sound. Tom stood next to the girl at the wheel as they cleared the harbour arm.

'What colour would you call your ship?' Tom asked, looking out of the window.

'She's a boat, not a ship, and she's pea-green; she's my beautiful pea-green boat,' said Tabitha, the girl like a cat.

'Tuwoo,' said the owl from his perch.

They were soon on the open sea. There was a swell in the water but the little green boat rode the waves easily enough, while her engine chugged, putt putt putt, and the moon rose and shone brightly above them so that Tom and Jollity were able to watch the Land of Stories as it got smaller and smaller, and further and further away behind them. After a while the faint harbour lights vanished altogether and they were finally out in the middle of the wide dark sea with no land visible in any direction.

'Wonder when we will be back?' Tom said.

'Time will tell, Tom,' said Jollity, lifting his wings and settling close against Tom's neck, for there was a chill in the air now.

'Have you been out of the Land of Stories before?' Tabitha asked.

'Yes,' Tom said. 'Just a few weeks ago we were away adventuring in the Land of Dark Stories.'

'Scary place for some,' said Tabitha, and she hummed a tune. 'From what I have heard they say the northern part of the place you are heading for now is, if anything, even scarier. You must be a very brave boy. Are you on a special mission for the sprites or the Master himself or something?'

'My mission is my own and is personal and secret,' said Tom tapping his nose. 'I am the youngest of the last ever adventuring family, and you might say I am on an urgent family mission. It was all my own idea, with a bit of help from an old friend, who is a senior sprite.'

'Well, Tom, my brave young adventurer, I should tuck yourself into bed soon; we'll most likely be sailing all through the night in any case.'

'Very well, Tabitha, goodnight then,' said Tom.

'Goodnight, Tom,' said Tabitha, 'and goodnight to you, my fine bird,' she added, looking at Jolliity with her big green eyes.

'Cawark,' Jollity said. There was something perhaps a little *too* catlike about pretty Tabitha for him, and he shivered his feathers as Tom went down the steps into the lower cabin.

The big brown owl was dozing on a perch near the bunk where Tom was to sleep. 'Tuwoo,' he cooed, 'tuwoo,' as Tom climbed under the sheets, as if he were saying a friendly goodnight.

'Not a bad sort, that owl,' said Jollity as he settled himself on the post at the end of the bunk.

'Goodnight, Jollity,' Tom said.

'Goodnight, Tom,' said Jollity, 'sweet dreams.'

Tom lay awake for a while listening to Tabitha busying herself about on deck. And later in the cabin, 'Goodnight, Owly-wowly dear,' he heard her say at one point and again the owl cooed out a 'tuwoo'.

While Tom settled himself to sleep he tried to picture the kindly face of his father, the man he had finally met in the great dark castle in the Land of Dark Stories. Try as he might he could only remember little bits of him. Kindly crinkle-edged blue eyes, a nose like Jacques's, a pair of gold glasses, strong fingers. After all, Tom thought, I was only the size of a thumb at the time, and his father's face had loomed up over him like the moon, so it had been hard to take it all in. In the end he gave up trying; he would know him when he saw him again. He was soon lulled by the rocking movement of the boat and the putt putt putt of the little engine and finally drifted into a dreamless sleep.

Tom was snapped awake by the loud, almost alarm-like, hooting of the big brown owl and the sudden dramatic lurches in the motion of the little pea-green boat. Jollity rose up into the air flapping his wings and he flew around the cabin calling out, 'We're sinking, look at those waves, it's a storm, a tempest.' The boat was going up and down, up and down.

Tom leapt out of the bunk and was almost imme-diately knocked back on to the decking by the pitch and roll of the boat.

He picked himself up and, holding on tight to the brass rail by the bunk, struggled into his adventurer's things. When he was dressed and equipped he clam-bered up the short steps on to the upper deck, with Jollity perched firmly on his shoulder.

Up on deck the wind and waves were reaching up above the boat and the sky was grey. The sea was no longer the gently swelling sapphire blue of the evening before. Now it was dark green, almost black, with bright white horses of wild foam blowing back across the bows of the little green boat.

Tabitha was struggling at the wheel. 'Sorry, young Tom,' she said, 'this is where we have to turn back.'

'Why?' Tom shouted over the wind.

'Dead ahead and north by north-east,' she said, 'whirlpool currents—see them?' She took one hand off the wheel and pointed.

Tom looked and could see some way off that the sea swirled round in a great spiral of waves and foam.

'Most likely a Kraken or a giant sea snake, one or the other. That's one of the dangers we face in these waters, like I said: mythical sea beasts. Look on the charts, it says on every one of them, "here be monsters", and there's your proof.'

'Can't we sail round it?' said Tom.

'Unfortunately we lost time in the night and we've been pushed off course. Too much wind to use the sails now and our fuel is low. If we go even a few sea yards closer we'll be sucked in and down, and worse. Have you ever seen a Kraken or a sea serpent?'

'No,' said Tom.

'Well, I have and you don't want to, Tom, believe me. You seem plucky enough for a young lad but even you aren't ready for either of those things.'

Tom grabbed hold of the rail, and turned his back to the sea. He could feel Jollity's claws gripping his shoulder.

'But I can't go back now! I will, I must, get to the Land of Myths and Legends,' he cried.

'Sorry, Tom, you'll be on your own then, for we have to turn back. It's not just the monsters, Tom, there's the time question as well,' Tabitha shouted back over the howling winds, 'the boundary sea . . . '

'What was that?' Tom shouted back.

Tabitha didn't hear him, and she turned and scanned the whirling water. Tom struggled back down into the cabin. The owl looked at him and blinked its big eyes. 'Tuwoo,' it said, 'tuwoo,' clinging on to its perch, rocking from side to side as the boat rode the big sea.

Tabitha came down in her yellow oilskins and

sou'wester hat. 'Now here's what you'll have to do,' she said.

'What?' Tom said. 'I'll do anything.'

'Bear in mind you will be on your own from now on. I had forgotten how bad and how dangerous these seas can be. First thing, I will need some more reward from you if I am to come back here later to pick you up.'

'I have nothing left,' said Tom, 'only my sword; I can't give you that.'

They stood together as the little boat rolled and pitched in the heavy sea. Tom held on to the edge of the chart table looking up at Tabitha in despair.

'I have a thought, Tom,' Tabitha said, taking pity on the pale boy in front of her. 'They say that there is any amount of sprite gold and all sorts of treasure over there in the Land of Myths. Find something and bring it back with you for me and if I think it is valuable enough we'll take you home.'

'I'll bring you back something special, don't worry,' Tom said firmly.

'Do you know, I think you will too, young Tom,' Tabitha said, showing her fine white teeth. 'Now,' she said, 'to work. Before we turn back I will launch our little lifeboat. It's a one man dinghy with a sail and oars. If you are prepared to take the risk you could take the long route past the whirlpool and then head inland. It will be very dangerous.'

'I don't mind danger,' said Tom, perhaps a little doubtfully. 'My brother Jake once took me out on the river and showed me what to do in a small boat, and how to use a sail and everything,' he said.

'Are you sure your rowing skills are up to it, Tom?' said Jollity, his head on one side.

'Now that's a wise bird,' Tabitha said, clutching the chart table as the boat lurched again, 'you listen to him. A river is nothing compared to that wild sea out there.'

'Jollity is very wise,' said Tom, his boots slipping now on the wet cabin floor.

'Well, that's it, we are shipping water, we have to drop you here and right now,' Tabitha said. 'We are at the boundary sea and must act before it's too late.'

'I'm ready,' said Tom.

'You're sure, Tom?' said Jollity.

'Sure,' said Tom.

Tabitha quickly studied the chart on the table.

'Look, Tom, we will wait for you here, in this very sea way off the Land of Myths and Legends. I will wait for you near this big rock formation. It is an island, really, it forms a bay and there is shelter there. You can see it marked on the chart just before the boundary sea.' She pointed it out to Tom. 'We will return near these mythical waters in a month's time. Do you think that will be long enough for your mission?'

'I hope so,' said Tom. 'I will need to find a vessel to take me there,' marking the island on his own map. 'What do you think?'

'You will have our little dinghy; hide it on the shore, and go back to it.'

'It's your mission, Tom,' said Jollity.

'We will wait, but only within reason.'

'I will make sure of your reward,' said Tom, 'you have my word as an Adventuring Trueheart.'

Chapter 5

The little wooden dinghy was lowered halfway to the waves. Tom clambered down into it. Jollity flew around his head. Tom settled on the seat and braced himself with the oars for the plunge into the raging sea. As soon as the little dinghy hit the waves Tom bravely pulled on the oars. Once he had his rhythm going he was able to slowly pull away from the side of the pea-green boat, but it was very hard work and he was soon soaked in salt spray. Jollity sat for a moment on the prow of the dinghy, doing his best to look like a carved figurehead, but the sea proved too strong for him. It kept leaping up and crashing over the prow so Jollity flew off into the wind and watched as the bigger boat pulled away back towards the Land of Stories. Tom waved goodbye to Tabitha, the 'Cat', as best he could while trying to keep hold of the oars.

She waved back to him and shouted over the wind, 'Go well, Tom; look after the boat, find me something special, and I hope we see you in a month,' and then the vessel turned away from Tom and the whirlpool.

Tom did his best, he rowed hard for a slight boy, and he rowed as well as he could, but it was heavy going. The seas were terrible. Salt water slapped him around the face with every stroke of the oars. The salt stung his eyes continually so that he could hardly see anything, or even where he was going. The storm seemed to be getting worse too. He was only just aware of the edge of the raging whirlpool. He did his best to keep away from it but the roaring noise just got louder and louder. Every time he lifted his head the swirling spiral of dark water seemed much closer. He was aware of Jollity shrieking something at him over the noise of the wind and sea. He felt a sudden pain in his shoulder as Jollity was forced to dig his claws in.

'You are getting nearer to that awful thing,' Jollity shouted. 'Come on, heave, Tom, heave, in out, that's it, pull away. Come on, Tom, you can do it, pull away harder.'

'Jollity, old friend,' Tom shouted, 'I don't think I can.'

Tom let the oars fall across his lap and he rested his arms for a moment.

'What are you doing, Tom, look, you're drifting in,' Jollity shrieked again over the howling winds.

Jollity could hear something else, something very odd. It was a soothing sweet sound floating over the rushing wind and churning waves. It was singing, and it sounded like girls' voices; there were no words, just a series of sweet high notes, and it was having a very strange effect on Tom.

'I must rest, must rest . . . arms,' Tom mumbled, his head suddenly dropping forwards.

The crow flew up, alarmed, and looked over the churning water. The whirlpool was getting closer every second but he couldn't see where the voices might be coming from. Tom looked as if he was suddenly fast asleep. The oars had dropped from his hands, and his head had fallen on to his chest.

Jollity dived down and flew about Tom's head. He flapped his wings hard and fanned at Tom's face. He pecked at him sharply with his beak, trying his best to wake him up. It was no good. Tom was slumped over in the seat with a smile on his face, as if he was safely tucked up in a cosy bed, having the most wonderful dream—instead of being a very small boy in a very small boat lost on a huge raging sea and heading fast into a dangerous whirlpool created by a mythical sea monster.

The boat spun round as the swirling water churned nearer and nearer to the dinghy. Jollity flew up once again in panic and alarm. He called out as loudly as he could manage to Tom, right in his ear, 'The whirlpool, Tom,' he cried. 'It's getting nearer. Come on, help, help yourself, get up, start rowing NOW! Come on, Tom, in, out, in, out.'

But Tom simply rolled around in his seat as the boat shifted in the sea. He looked like a rag doll version of himself, somehow, stuffed with straw, his arms flopped to his side, the oars clattered down at his feet.

The little boat was soon caught in the far edge of the spiral of churning dark water. So much water came flooding in over the little prow, and in such great foaming torrents that the boat sank lower and lower. The spiral rush moved the little boat round and round, faster and faster in the water. When Jollity flew up high again he could see down into the deep dark centre of the swirling whirlpool. He tried to steady himself, tried to hover in the raging wind. He could see huge green tentacles waving fathoms below in the water. A large eye stared up at him and at the little boat.

Now the boat itself was hanging, spinning round on the vertical wall of the furious giant whirlpool and Jollity could see that soon Tom and the boat would be gone, lost for ever in the terrible deep.

Chapter 6

A black airship floated across the cold seas near the Land of Myths and Legends. It had a white skull and crossbones painted along its sides. Some sailors looked up and saw it pass over through the drifts of falling snow and they called out in fear to the heavens. The airship passed gracefully over the land and floated across miles of dense pine forest. A farmer in his snow-covered field saw the dark ship as it crossed the sky. He fell to his knees and covered his head with his cowl in terror. The airship finally landed, gently nudging a cloudfall of soft snow from a stand of trees. A figure emerged, jumped down on to the ground and secured a rope tether to the solid trunk of one of the trees. He was a tall man and his face looked as if it had been stitched together from all sorts of other faces. Once the airship was settled, two passengers emerged shivering from the cabin. They were Julius Ormestone, the self-styled king of the Land of Dark Stories, and his prisoner, Big Jack Trueheart, father of Tom, and also, of course, of Jack, Jake, Jacques, Jackson, Jackie, and Jacquot.

Big Jack's hands were bound together and he was joined to Ormestone by a length of sprite chain.

A third passenger, a hunched little sprite, slipped unseen by the others from the back of the airship's gondola roof where he had hidden himself for the whole of the long flight. He was Rumpelstiltskin, a thwarted figure, who was in love with all the Trueheart brothers' princess brides. He had once been Ormestone's own right-hand sprite, and was a weaver of usefully powerful sprite spells. Ormestone had promised him the hands of all the princesses in marriage, but Ormestone had betrayed Rumpelstiltskin, and Rumpelstiltskin had in turn sworn to get vengeance. Rumpelstiltskin quickly hid himself again, among some tall pine trees at the edge of the forest. It was not the right time to reveal himself just yet. He would have to be patient. His revenge against his old master was a long-term thing which needed careful planning. His chance would surely come; until then he would have to be content to watch and wait and perhaps interfere secretly when neccessary.

Ormestone left the stitched-faced man to guard the airship and set off on foot taking Big Jack with him. A village of friendly looking white houses stood a mile or so off from the forest by a nearby lake at the bottom of a steep-sided mountain. Ormestone stopped halfway and sniffed the air suddenly. 'Mmm,' he said, 'I smell sulphur, and where there is sulphur there are mythic dragons, and where there are mythic dragons there is also . . . ' he paused and then said his favourite word in a shivery whisper . . . 'gold.'

The lake was dark and unnaturally still; it was frozen over and looked like black glass. Big Jack burrowed his head further into his collar against the freezing wind. The wind strangely enough did nothing to ruffle the surface of the water. The little village seemed quiet and peaceful. Ormestone hammered on the door of the nearest and largest of the houses. The door opened a crack and a short fair-haired man put his head out and looked at Ormestone. But without speaking, he quickly put his head back in and shut the door.

Ormestone banged again, and kept banging.

A worried face appeared at the window nearest the door, and then it too quickly disappeared again.

'We are lost travellers,' Ormestone called out. 'We seek something to eat and drink; we ask only for just a *little* of your hospitality.'

The door opened again a little wider this time and the same man appeared, holding an axe almost as big as himself.

'Good morning, sir,' said Ormestone smiling one of his creepy smiles. 'I am a king in exile and this gentleman is my prisoner. Have no fear for he is not dangerous, just a poor misguided soul. We have travelled for many days and nights and are in need only of some simple fare, some bread and water, whatever you have that you can spare.'

The man ushered them inside warily, still clutching his axe, his eyes narrowed.

'You may share some alebrod with me,' he said gruffly. 'My name is Uhn, I am . . . the watcher,' he added importantly and then he bowed to show proper respect.

'I am King Ormestone from a . . . far land,' said Ormestone vaguely, puffing himself up as tall as he could. 'What is it that you watch, Mr Uhn?'

Uhn bowed even lower. 'If it please your majesty, I watch the forest and I watch the skies for the safety of our village,' he said. 'I have heard of a prophecy fulfilled just earlier today. Folkmar the farmer saw a black ship up in the sky; it can only be a matter of time before another prophecy comes to pass as well.'

'Another prophecy?' said Ormestone.

'There are many prophecies,' said Uhn, his voice darkening and quivery. 'Why, the giant wolf of the forest, Fenrir, has been seen; add to that the black ship that sails the skies, and that can spell nothing but doom for us all,' Uhn added gloomily. 'Now, won't you sit and eat with me, sire?'

Ormestone sat himself down on a simple wooden chair. Big Jack stood near the door looking around the room. A long table was laid with a wooden bowl and a spoon, a bigger wooden bowl full of what looked like very dingy grey porridge, and next to it a wooden ladle. Uhn went to the cupboard and took out a similar wooden bowl.

He ladled some of the thick dingy porridge stuff into the bowl and pushed it across the table. 'Alebrod,' Uhn said, shaking his head miserably.

'A black ship in the sky, giant wolves, some sort of fairy tale surely?' Ormestone said hurriedly. 'Pray what is this alebrod that you offer us, Mr Uhn?'

'Old bread and old beer, waste not want not, with one or two tasty forest snails stirred in for flavour. It's what we eat here in the winter when the lake is frozen over, and we cannot fish,' Uhn said glumly. 'Will you feed your prisoner too, your highness?'

'I will presently,' said Ormestone, raising a spoonful of the thick alebrod to his mouth, 'but he must wait.'

From the darkness of the trees there came the sound of an unearthly howling.

Uhn stood and went over to the door, opened it a crack and looked out to the treeline, his axe held firmly in his hand.

'What is it?' said Ormestone.

'The very wolf I mentioned, the wolf that we all fear,' said Uhn, 'the wolf Fenrir.'

Ormestone clamped his thin slot of a mouth tight shut on the spoonful of alebrod. He chewed thoughtfully

47

and after a moment he looked as if he were chewing suddenly on a live wasp. His eyes widened and he stopped chewing; he had never in his life tasted anything so horrible. He could not allow his disgust to show, could not show any weakness to the peasant Uhn. Amongst the cloying sticky stale bread and the rancid ale he had detected something slimy, salty, and very slightly gritty. He had felt it crunch in his mouth, and it seemed to wriggle. He finally managed to swallow just one single bitter wet lump of the alebrod; he felt it slide down his throat. He was only just able to speak. 'I shall be a merciful king,' he said to Uhn, 'I shall offer this food to my prisoner here.' He pushed the bowl across to Big Jack. 'You may eat your fill.'

So Big Jack Trueheart, with his hands tied awkwardly together, was forced to attempt to eat the bowl of alebrod.

Ormestone, relieved, stood and looked out of the window. 'I cannot see any sign of a wolf,' he said.

'No one has ever seen it,' said Uhn in his doom-laden voice. 'It is famous in our mythology. It can see us, though. It will seek out and find the guilty, or the unworthy among us. Then it will tear them limb from limb, before they know what's hit them.'

'Really,' said Ormestone, 'how amusing.' But he shivered slightly in his cloak and went and warmed himself at the low fire with his back to the room.

Jack had manfully swallowed the rest of the alebrod. He took his chance and sneaked a little square of Trueheart cloth from under the cuff of his coat. He appeared to wipe his mouth with it and then dropped the piece of fabric into the empty wooden bowl.

Uhn sat back in his chair and lit up a little clay pipe. He let the smoke drift up.

Ormestone said, 'So far only two prohecies, Mr Uhn, there surely should be a third. Can't have things in twos, there must be three?'

'Oh, there is a third prophecy right enough,' said Uhn, 'and that's the one that might just be the saving of us all. Seen no sign though, no sign at all.'

'What is your third prophecy?'

'Why, the boy, of course, sire,' said Uhn. 'The boy warrior who is prophesied.'

Ormestone bristled a little, and looked over at Big Jack who just smiled back at him blankly.

'I see,' said Ormestone coldly, turning back. 'Tell me, did I smell the tell-tale smell of sulphur on the way here? Is there a dragon in the neighbourhood as well as your giant wolf?'

'Oh yes, sire, we do indeed have a dragon.'

'And,' said Ormestone, his eyes glittering, his sudden smile fixed, 'tell me more.'

'Our dragon lives up there in a deep cave in the mountain.' Uhn gestured with the stem of his pipe. 'We see the smoke sometimes, drifting out of the entrance.'

'Friendly or no?'

'We rarely see the great creature itself, sire,' said Uhn. 'It's never done us any harm so far; we leave it alone, it leaves us alone.' And he nodded his head.

Uhn took the wooden bowls and stacked them by the kitchen pump. He looked out of the window. 'By rights it should be our spring by now, sire. The meadow flowers should be out, but this awful thick snow and this freezing winter seems set in for good. Our lake is solid black ice and it's getting worse by the day. Some about here say 'tis the Fimbul, the mighty winter, and that Ragnarok will be coming, what with the omen of the black ship that has been seen in the sky, and the howling of the giant wolf.'

'Ragnarok?' said Ormestone.

'The end of days,' said Uhn, 'the end of all things, of our gods, the end of everything.'

'Really,' said Ormestone, through his horrible gash of a smile, 'fancy that. By the way, do you by any chance have a large bag or an old sack which we could have to help us on our journey?'

Once outside Uhn's house Ormestone pushed Big Jack Trueheart forward towards the lower slope of the mountain.

'When we're there I'll take the binding from your hands, you're going to need to use them. But remember, you'd best help me in any way I ask, and behave yourself, if you ever want to see your pathetic little Tom, and the rest of your feeble minded, blundering Trueheart family ever again.' And he laughed his nasty laugh.

As they walked they skirted the edge of the frozen lake, and just then came another huge piercing wolf howl from the darkness of the forest.

Ormestone stopped and looked back, and Big Jack noticed that Ormestone was distinctly nervous; the prophecy of the giant wolf had clearly got to him deep down in some way. Or perhaps, Jack thought, it was the prophecy of the boy?

Back at the tree line, Rumpelstiltskin, hidden among the tree trunks, raised an abandoned hunting horn that he had found to his mouth once more. He let out another of his blood curdling imitation wolf howls.

He knew his Norse legends well, and he also knew just how to play on his master's fears. The howling sounds would have been sure to set the peasant off prattling on about Fenrir, and Rumpelstiltskin knew how much the legend of Fenrir, the wolf that tore the guilty to pieces, might unsettle his master, and he wanted his old master to be as unsettled as possible. When he saw that Ormestone and Big Jack had reached the cave entrance he set off towards them swiftly across the snow.

At the entrance to the dragon's cave Ormestone untied Big Jack's hands. Jack shook his hands, and tried to warm them. An icy wind blew sharply from across the lake and fresh snow was falling.

'I like the sound of this Ragnarok business,' Ormestone muttered to himself. 'I really must encourage it. I like unhappy endings, and a final ending to everything is even better. It's just perfect, though I wonder why my airship should be part of their old prophecies?' He stopped and listened out for the wolf howl, but there was just the wind. The thought of the giant wolf that seeks out the guilty, the bad, the villainous, the unworthy, had got to him. However he must show no weakness in front of a Trueheart.

Big Jack shook his head and sighed. His fingers were just warming up, some feeling was returning to them, and as he felt a welcome surge of strength, the possibility of getting away crossed his mind. Perhaps it was because he had noticed that sudden look of fear and uncertainty that crossed Ormestone's face when he had heard the giant wolf howl that Jack felt suddenly confident of an escape. There was, however, the question of the long sprite chain which attached him to Ormestone; he would need to find a way to break it.

Rumpelstiltskin followed them. He had cloaked himself in his own sprite-made mist which gave him near invisibility. He kept himself hidden near the cave entrance among the rough frosted gorse that covered the lower slopes of the mountain.

'Somewhere in this darkness will be the dragon,' Ormestone whispered. 'Your job will be to distract it sufficiently so that I can get in and take away its hoard of gold.'

'Not possible,' said Big Jack quietly, 'I am after all unarmed.' He spread his arms wide.

'Strange, I thought you were an adventurer, and therefore resourceful. I thought you were big, bold, clever, and brave. Use your head, serve your purpose, and I will keep you alive. Use your brains, if you have any. Improvise, man,' Ormestone whispered as he pushed Jack into the entrance of the cave. He followed some way behind, allowing the sprite chain, which was easily lengthened or shortened, to stretch out. The smell of sulphur mixed in with an all round foul stench of decaying and rotten matter grew worse the further into the cave they went. The floor of the cave sloped upwards quite steeply for several yards and where it crested there was a steep drop down. Below was a greenish glow of light and a noisy throb, a regular rumbling thunderous sound. Jack went to the edge of the rock path and looked down over the edge.

Chapter 7

HAFNIR THE BOLD, SIGURD THE SLY, AND
THE BOY WHO WAS PROPHESIED 10.43 P.M.

Hafnir, son of Hafnir, sometimes known as Hafnir the Bold, stood in the prow of his warship. He wore on his head a winged helmet of beaten copper. A grey wolf pelt was draped across his broad shoulders and a round wooden shield edged with bright copper bolts was strapped across his back. In the centre of the shield was the likeness of a large wolf worked in thin sprite gold. Hafnir had two thick lumps of cork and wax torn from an old ale jar stuffed into each of his ears. He was defying the sirens.

He was sailing his dragon-prowed war vessel as close as he dared to the Kraken's whirlpool. He had sailed his vessel like this in this raging sea for as many years as he had been a warrior.

'Blow winds, sing, foul sirens, for I cannot hear you. I will sail across your path, monster of the deep, and I dare you to try and stop me,' he shouted into the wind. 'We will complete our purpose.'

They had already seen one prophecy come true with the sighting of the strange black flying ship in the sky some days before; it could surely only be a matter of time before there was another.

Hafnir's crew all had their ears stuffed with bits of cork and wax too, and so the sirens' song did not affect them either. Some worked the sail, while the others rowed the long oars, and pulled hard against the spinning whirlpool of dark grey-green sea. Every day and every night they patrolled the storming seas according to their instructions.

Hafnir took his bull's horn from around his neck as they once more crossed the treacherous great swirl of water and blew a huge triumphant blasting note out into the wind. At that moment Jollity flew up above the ship shrieking out what would have sounded to Hafnir like, 'Help help', if he hadn't closed his ears to the sirens' song.

Hafnir saw the black bird suddenly rise up from the depths of the whirlpool. Aha, he thought, here, perhaps, finally, was the omen.

He leaned over the side of his ship and looked down into the foaming waters and he saw a small boat. Nothing more than a dinghy, and it was held tight in the slimy Kraken's tentacle. He could also see a young boy, dressed in the cloak and buckskins of a hunter or an adventurer. He was lying dazed, and almost submerged in the water which flooded the boat.

The boy of the prophecy.

At least, this looked very likely to be him; how else to explain the black bird, the crow, his expected familiar, this far out into mythical waters.

The omen must always be respected.

Hafnir wasted no time. He grabbed his first mate, Sigurd, and gestured down to the boy in the boat. Sigurd's eyes widened and then he fell on his knees and his eyes turned heavenward. Hafnir picked him up and shook him and then he tied a length of rough hawser rope about himself and secured one end quickly with a powerful knot to the the thick neck of the dragon prow. He indicated to Sigurd that he was going, and then he jumped over the side of his vessel. He let himself fall all the way down on to the little dinghy.

The crow flew around his head. It was calling out something, but of course Hafnir's ears were stopped up so he could hear nothing but the dull rumble and roaring of the wind and the sea. Hafnir landed four square on his big booted feet in the flooded little boat. The Kraken's huge slimy tentacle, which was a brackish green colour and covered in polyps, shells, and suckers, was quickly tightening around the hull of the dinghy. Soon the little boat and everything in it would be crushed and dragged below the waves; there was no time to lose. Hafnir grabbed the boy up in his arms and then tugged hard on the thick rope.

Sigurd, standing amazed in the prow of the bigger ship, quickly hauled Hafnir and the boy up from the little swamped craft just as the Kraken's tentacles finally crushed everything and pulled the fragments down into the depths.

Hafnir's proud dragon ship sailed majestically across the centre of the Kraken's raging whirlpool. The hideous creature below tugged once or twice at the ship with one of its tentacles, but the combination of wind and sail, and the strength of the oarsmen was too powerful even for such supernatural force.

Hafnir's war vessel turned in a sudden wide curve away from the whirlpool. The line of copper shields caught the moonlight and flashed with pale fire, and a great cheer went up from the warrior crew. Hafnir pulled the cork and wax plugs from his ears and shook his head. Sigurd did the same, and they both looked down at Tom lying dizzy and wet on the deck.

Tom sat up slowly; his head spun and cold sea water dripped from his wild hair. He looked up at the looming figures of Hafnir and Sigurd.

'Who are you?' Tom asked warily, as if he had just woken from a dream, looking from one to the other.

'I could ask you the same question,' said Hafnir in a deep and booming, but not unfriendly voice, 'but then I have no need to, for I know who you are. I am Hafnir the Bold, and I just plucked you free, my young 'un, but inches from the very Kraken itself.'

'Yes, young master,' said Sigurd nodding, 'right from the terrible whirlpool in the seas. The omens were seen too, the black ship in the sky, and the black crow, the forest bird, the night-black bird flying far out at sea, as was foretold, the dark harbingers.'

'That would be Jollity, my crow,' said Tom. 'Where is he, and come to that, where am I?'

'You are safely landed now on the honoured deck of my vessel,' said Hafnir. 'She is named *Dragon Helm Twenty Oars*, may her sails catch the winds. But wait, where are my manners? First things first, you'd best come with me and dry yourself, young master.'

At the rear of the ship an iron brazier stood balanced on a square metal shield; it was filled with glowing hot coals. Tom sat on a chest decorated with the likeness of a wolf all worked in beaten sprite gold which stood next to the brazier. He was shivering now and trying to warm himself. The swirling whirlpool waters were far behind them, and he imagined that a dark and rocky coastline would soon appear.

'Are you telling us that you personally know that dark bird of omen?' asked Sigurd.

'Yes,' said Tom, 'he's my travelling companion.'

Sigurd nodded his head. 'You must be a very great hero to travel with an omen bird of your very own,' he whispered.

'I am Tom Trueheart,' said Tom, 'of the Adventuring Truehearts.'

'It is him, I am sure he is the one,' Hafnir whispered under his breath to Sigurd.

'I am on a mission,' Tom continued, 'to find and rescue . . . ' and here he hesitated, 'to find and rescue . . . someone important to me who is lost somewhere in the Land of Myths and Legends.'

'This misson of yours,' said Hafnir very quietly, 'would it have anything to do with a Dark King in exile?'

Sigurd shook his head as if the very mention of the Dark King was troubling, and before Tom had a chance to answer, Jollity flew down and landed on Tom's shoulder. Hafnir and Sigurd both stepped back away from the brazier and stood looking over in fear at Tom and the bird outlined against the flames. The bird looked at the two warriors then lowered his own head and still keeping them firmly in his gaze said suddenly and loudly, 'Squark.' Sigurd jumped a little and clutched hold of Hafnir's arm.

'It's all right, Jollity,' said Tom, 'they are friends. They just rescued me from a sea monster.'

'I know that, Tom,' said Jollity, 'I was just making sure of them.'

'The harbinger doth speak to us,' said Hafnir, and he fell at once on one knee and bowed his head.

'It's all right, really,' said Tom, 'don't be afraid.'

'We are very afraid,' said Hafnir.

'But you rescued me,' said Tom puzzled.

'You were about to go under the waves,' said Hafnir. 'The little boat was in the grip of the tentacles of a fierce and terrible sea monster.'

'And you weren't scared of that,' said Tom, 'but you are of Jollity here?'

'Sea monsters are no problem for us. Our good ship and our noble warriors deal with them daily,' said Sigurd. 'It's the omens and prophecies, and what they could mean. The omens could signal the very end of days, which we call Ragnarok. This would mean the end of all the gods and of all of us, *that's* what frightens us. We have already seen the black ship in the sky that warns of a Dark King in exile, a cruel king who comes from the sky.' And here Sigurd bowed his head once more.

Tom had an idea exactly who this Dark King might be.

'This king of yours,' said Tom, 'is he a tall fellow, wearing black, with a head of white hair, by name Ormestone?'

Hafnir almost pushed the wax plugs back into his ears. 'Say not a name, young hero, say it not.'

'That name may well be cursed,' said Sigurd.

'I know him all right,' said Tom. 'You see, he has hold of my father, Big Jack Trueheart the Giant Killer, a good man and a noble adventurer who was lost to us these many years. The king has taken him and it is my mission to find my father and rescue him and I must not fail, I will not fail. All I ask of you is that you might drop me ashore somewhere so that I can start my quest.'

'That is exactly what we must do,' said Hafnir. 'That is the true meaning of our own quest: our mission was to find you. We sail the seas daily and now we have found you. You see, you are the boy who was prophesied. You are vital to us and our people and we will help you in any and every way we can, for you will defeat the darkness and the winter. This long, long winter is all part of the same prophecy. It is still snowing and it should not be; we fear that this could be the "Fimbul" the mighty and eternal and final winter, the signal of Ragnarok.' And he shook his head.

Sigurd put his hand on Hafnir's shoulder. He turned to Tom and said, 'We must rely on you now, you are the boy who was prophesied. We must rely on your courage, and on your wisdom; it could be that only you can stop Ragnarok.'

'Who is this Ragnarok?' said Tom.

'Why,' said Hafnir, 'Ragnarok is not a person, it is an event, the end of days, the end of everything, the end of this our world, just as it has been prophesied.'

Chapter 8

INSIDE THE DRAGON'S CAVE

Big Jack looked down and saw the huge slumbering shape of a dragon. Its leathery wings were folded back and its long scaly neck was lying low along the murky floor of the cave. As far as Jack could tell its eyes were closed. Little puffs and wisps of stinking green smoke came from its nostrils as it breathed, along with loud deep rumbling noises. A dark pool of underground water lapped at its webbed and clawed front feet which were crossed under its enormous snout. The snout was studded with the tips of gleaming white teeth. The teeth stuck up this way and that along the jawline. It was a fearsome beast. Visible, piled under its green scaly body on either side, catching the light, were glimpses of gold, a huge mound of flickering gold coins.

Ormestone was soon beside Jack. 'There it is,' he whispered excitedly, his eyes widening, 'sprite gold, just what I need. Now move that dragon away, distract it.'

'How am I supposed to do that?' Jack whispered.

'You'll think of something,' Ormestone said in a quiet and menacing voice. 'If you don't I shall be forced to act against your best interests and we wouldn't want that, would we. Think if you will of poor Mrs Trueheart all alone at night in the house in the forest. I have only to send an urgent message to the right people and . . . need I say any more?'

'Not a word,' said Jack and then he picked his way forward down the slope below the crest of rock, all the way down towards where the dragon lay snoozing. The sprite chain spooled out behind him, and it scraped and rattled over the rocks as he descended. The dragon seemed to stir in its sleep; the smoke came out of its nostrils in a longer stream. The rumbling noise stopped for an instant. Jack stopped too and held his breath. He looked around for possible quick escape routes; not from Ormestone, but from the dragon.

The path he was on skirted the pool of dark water. Then it twisted and climbed again further into the dark of the mountain. If he had to run suddenly, he noticed that there was a narrow entrance higher up, back through the rock, which he hoped the dragon would be too big to fit through. Jack thought that there was enough slack in the chain to allow for such an escape. He felt his chain tighten suddenly, as if he were a common dog being brought to heel by a strict master. He looked back at Ormestone who urged him on, gesturing with his hand, waving the empty sack, the other hand pulling on the sprite chain. Jack had to do something, and now.

Rumpelstiltskin eased himself through the cave entrance and worked his way quietly forwards. He could see his old master, Ormestone, outlined against a green glow and waving an empty sack above his head. A sack for stealing the gold hoard no doubt, Rumpelstiltskin thought. The leopard doesn't change his spots. He dodged between lumps and fissures of rock. He could smell the sulphurous smell of dragon, and with dragon always came the hoard, the hoard of gold. Keeping to the shadows he worked his way to the edge and looked down. Sure enough an enormous dragon lay slumbering and Big Jack Trueheart stood too near its head, with his arm raised up. He was holding a big rock. Rumpelstiltskin had a choice to make. He could stand in the shadows and watch Big Jack get spit-roasted and barbecued by the dragon or he could intervene and help Jack, who would at some point in the future become a useful ally against Ormestone. Rumpelstiltskin was after all playing the long game. He's going to need my sprite magic and right away, by the look of it, Rumpelstiltskin thought.

Jack selected a loose chunk of rock from the floor of the cave. He weighed it in his hand, and briefly looked back at Ormestone who pointed at the dragon and nodded. Jack thought that he saw a familiar small hunched figure flicker and move back into the shadows, on the far side of the rock ridge, but he shook his head and dismissed the idea as a trick of the light. Then he threw the rock as hard as he could at the dragon's snout.

The rock hit the dragon. Its eye opened slowly, drowsily at first. The eye was a deep livid green colour with a vertical iris like a lizard's. The iris widened, sucking in the light. Then the dragon slowly opened its other eye. It glared at Jack. Jack picked up another rock and threw it and it bounced off the dragon's snout again. The dragon raised its long neck and then stood up to its full height. The green eyes fixed Jack in their sights and then the dragon opened its mouth wide.

After Big Jack threw the second rock there was no point in waiting around; he knew exactly what would happen next. He ran up the narrow side path to the small tunnel entrance on the other side of the cave. He heard an enormous roar behind him and then the darkness was broken by a huge ball of fire which lit up the whole of the cave in a flash of yellow and orange light. Jack saw his shadow suddenly flare up on the path in front of him and he dived to the ground as a wave of hot gas, flame, and stinking sulphurous smoke flew over him. He picked himself up and staggered on through the choking smoke. A second roar filled his ears. Another bright orange flash lit the cave interior. Jack ran as fast as he could towards where he hoped the narrow entrance would be; he could no longer see it through all the smoke. The dragon followed him. It raised itself off the ground with its leathery wings and flew a little way, coughing out angry fireballs.

Jack clambered up the among the rocks towards the tunnel entrance, which looked much bigger the closer he got to it. He panicked, perhaps the dragon would fit through it after all?

There was another roar and another burst of bright light behind him. The dragon was very close. Jack was stuck between rocks. He couldn't quite reach the next set of handholds and the sprite chain seemed to have either run out or be caught on something among the rocks which kept him held back. He turned his head to see the dragon hovering very close to him, its wings beating slowly. Its green eyes were wide open and staring down at him. Its long snout was lifted and its cheeks were puffed out, storing another searing blast of gas, flame, and smoke, which would now surely finish him off, roast him into charred, barbecued cinders in the next second.

As soon as the dragon set off to chase after Big Jack Trueheart, Ormestone slithered down the path. He splashed happily through the lapping dark water of the pool, and climbed up, his feet slipping and sliding, on to the hoard of gold coins. Beautiful ancient coins they were too, heavy and slightly misshapen, great solid lumps of pure sprite gold. There was a bursting flash of yellow light in the cavern and the coins shone suddenly as the great mound reflected the radiant light and heat in a million golden sparks and flashes. Ormestone almost cried for joy at the weight and sight of all the coins. He lost no time, and as a second flash and roar rolled and filled the dark cave he began to scoop the coins into the sack.

Rumpelstiltskin edged forward. He feared that Jack had seen him earlier, but no matter, his sprite powers were needed now. The dragon was poised in the air, hovering above the scrambling figure of Big Jack Trueheart; it was preparing to roast him. This did not fit in with the plan at all; Rumpelstiltskin had other long-term ideas. He pointed his twig wand at the dragon.

Try as it might, it seeemed that the dragon suddenly could not open its mouth at all. It tried to release a deadly fireball but nothing came out but a puff of smoke. Its eyes narrowed. Jack scrambled down from the rock and ran back up the scorched path as the dragon turned awkwardly in the air, and bumped its bulky body against the roof of the cave. This dislodged some great lumps of reddish rock which crashed down on to its wings. The dragon slumped to the ground. It managed to let some of the gas and flame out through its nostrils but not enough to affect Jack. The dragon craned its neck forward and blew another gust of flame through its nostrils. The flames lit up the scene. Ormestone was running too; he had helped himself to all the precious gold, piece by piece, and piled it into a sack.

Ormestone turned, saw that the dragon had noticed him, and set off at once, dragging the heavy sack of gold with him. The dragon flew towards where the precious gold hoard had been, while Jack ran as low to the ground as he could, back to Ormestone.

Rumpelstiltskin saw all this from his vantage point, saw that the furious dragon, though still struggling to expel flame and gas, was dangerous and gaining on

Ormestone. Much as he would like to see Ormestone consumed in a ball of dragon flame, he had other plans. It was time to slow the dragon down. He pointed his sprite wand again and the dragon almost came to a halt in mid air. Its wings slowed; it looked as if it was suddenly flying through treacle. Puffs of green smoke and little parps of angry flame shot out of its nostrils but not enough to reach either Jack or Ormestone. Ormestone reeled in Jack's chain and Jack stumbled up the path.

'Carry that outside,' Ormestone cried pointing to the bulging sack. Jack heaved the heavy sack of gold out through the cave entrance. Ormestone was soon behind him. 'Back to the airship,' he shouted. 'Something was wrong with that dragon, but we are not waiting around to find out what it was.'

Rumpelstiltskin came out a moment later, wrapped in his cold cloak of mist. They did not see him as he hurried behind them back to the airship, the black ship of the sky. He knew they didn't have long, the spell would wear off soon enough, and when it did there would be one very, very angry dragon left for the poor locals to deal with.

Chapter 9

Hafnir said to Tom, 'Now you are rested, and look how dawn lights the sky, I think the time has come, young master adventurer.' And he blew loudly on his bull horn so that the rising notes sounded above the winds and the sea.

'We head back now,' he said. 'We shall take you to the Norse Lands and put you ashore.'

Tom could see a shoreline in the faint light, suddenly emerging from the scattered snow and mist.

Once they neared land Tom could see tall conical

mountains with snow caps and thick drifts of snow on the slopes. Beneath them and running down to the shore was an enormous forest of dark green, almost black, pine trees. It was a little like the eastern forest in the Land of Stories, only much bigger, much darker, and it seemed to stretch on forever. The rocks themselves looked like the twisted flow of some thick liquid that had simply stopped and frozen in an instant. Which is just what the rocks were: volcanic lava that had been stopped cold in its tracks. There was a steep-sided inlet of dark water with rocky outcrops and islands standing tall, and sheer walls of icy-looking rock on either side, as if the land had been sliced into like some iced-over birthday cake.

'The fjords and inlets of our beautiful homeland,' said Hafnir, with a sigh. 'We will put you ashore some way up the misty river.' He looked up at the sky and the scattered flakes of snow.

'I am only an apprentice adventurer,' said Tom nervously. 'I am the youngest of the Truehearts, the last adventuring family; I'm not sure what I can do to help.'

'You are the boy in the prophecy. A prophecy that

has been handed down to us,' said Hafnir. 'We are all relying on you.'

'You must succeed,' said Sigurd quietly, looking up at the high snow-covered rocks.

'It's all right, Tom,' said Jollity quietly. 'Come on now; with a true heart, we'll pull through somehow.'

The good ship *Dragon Helm Twenty Oars* anchored at the inlet. Tom was about to be lowered down on to the icy shore when Hafnir said, 'Wait, I have something important for you.' He opened the chest that stood near the brazier, reached into it and pulled out a black winter cloak. It was lined and edged with thick grey fur. 'This is another important part of our prophecy. This gift has been waiting for you, our chosen hero. The fur that you see here is a small part clipped by an older hero in the time of heroes. It was bravely trimmed by sword from the living pelt of Fenrir, the wolf of the gods. Wear this against the cold, and it will, of course, keep you warm, and ours is a cold land. You will find that it will protect you in other ways too. It could save you from Fenrir the wolf himself, and it can also ward off blows from swords, axes, hammers, almost anything,' Hafnir said. 'It is a magical cloak and one fit for a hero. It might well save your life and your quest one day, so wear it well.'

Tom said, 'Thank you,' and took the cloak and wrapped it at once around his shoulders. It fitted so well it seemed to have been made for him. Jollity flew over and landed on the branch of a tall pine.

'Goodbye then, young master,' said Hafnir.

'Go with the gods,' said Sigurd, and patted Tom on the shoulder.

'Goodbye,' said Tom. 'Thank you for rescuing me. I will do my best to help with this Ragnarok.'

'We can ask no more of you,' said Hafnir.

Tom was lowered down on to the twisted rocks. Jollity flew across and settled on his shoulder.

The ship weighed anchor. An archer stood on the high part of the deck and fired a flaming arrow which arced through the air and landed on a lone pine tree high among the rocks above the inlet. The little tree suddenly caught fire and burned brightly in the cold air, and Hafnir called out, 'The fire marks the beginning of your path, follow it, young master, and farewell.'

Tom waved back to Hafnir and Sigurd as the ship sailed away back up the inlet to the open sea.

Tom set his face inland. Jollity said, 'This is a strange looking land indeed.'

'And a very, very cold one, too,' said Tom shivering, grateful for the warmth of his new cloak.

Chapter 10

ACROSS THE COLD AND MYTHIC LAND

8.17 A.M.

The path took Tom and Jollity past the burning pine tree to a high plateau. Here they had a view of the whole country for miles ahead. The treeline stopped far away in the distance and there was a sudden emptier landscape beyond the forest. It seemed to be made of the same twisted volcanic rock all covered over with yellow lichen, and patched with snow, which fell thick and fast. The deep forest stretched ahead of them, and far off in the distance Tom could see a lake and a simple village of what looked like white houses with friendly looking smoke curling up above them. 'A good place to shelter and study the map,' said Tom.

Tom walked the winding path down to the forest, while Jollity flew overhead keeping an eye on things. At several points as he walked sudden geysers of hot water shot out of rock pools high into the air. There were deep looking, black iced-over pools, and even a frozen waterfall of ice crystals which cascaded down the sheer rock face. 'This is a wild and worrying sort of place, Tom,' said Jollity.

'We've seen worse,' said Tom bravely, but he pulled the wolf cloak closer about him all the same as they finally entered the edge of the dark forest.

The snow lay thick on the ground, even under the trees. It was slow work trudging along under the low dark branches. Great clumps of snow would suddenly fall from the trees making a 'whump' sound and Tom jumped every time: to him it sounded like the footfall of a troll or some other giant creature. There were other strange noises too, skitterings and snapping twigs all round them. And then there were some distant but

83

loud howlings, which sounded unmistakably like wolves.

'I don't like the sound of that,' Tom said, stopping in his tracks and listening.

'Nor do I, Tom,' said Jollity, and the crow took off at once and flew up above the treeline.

Jollity soon returned and settled on Tom's shoulder, shaking and shivering.

'I thought I saw a wolf, Tom, some way ahead.'

'What was the name of that special wolf they mentioned?'

'Fenrir,' said Jollity.

'Which way should we go to avoid it then?' Tom said.

'I saw the wolf over in that direction,' Jollity said, pointing his black wing.

'Then we will go this way,' said Tom and set off to walk in the opposite direction with Jollity firmly perched on his shoulder.

For a while as they walked through the snow all was quiet; there were no more howls from any wolves. But then there was a build-up of faint skitterings and scamperings. There were the sounds of soft footfalls, the padding of paws over snow. The sounds seemed to come from all around them, inching closer. Jollity flew up again for a look. He circled the trees and then came back.

'We're surrounded, Tom,' he said. 'Wolves, they've crept up on us, dozens of them.'

'Do you think they're Ormestone's minions?' Tom said, reaching for his sword.

'I don't think so, Tom, just look through there.' The crow raised a wing and pointed ahead through the dense tree trunks.

All Tom could see through the falling snow was a grey blur just ahead through the trees. The grey blur howled and the trees shook and more snow fell from the branches.

Tom let go of his sword. 'Fenrir,' he whispered.

'Afraid so, Tom,' Jollity said.

They moved forward very slowly. Tom was conscious of every footfall as his boots sank into the thick snow. The grey blur became clearer. Tom saw a pair of yellow eyes staring down at him from some way up, as if the wolf was standing high up in a tree.

The wolf wasn't standing in a tree. It was just very

tall. The eyes fixed on Tom and seemed to brighten in intensity. Other, smaller, wolves were closer to them now, surrounding them in a wide circle and staring silently.

Tom finally stopped in his tracks and Jollity flew up to a nearby branch.

The lone wolf stepped heavily forward through the snow and its outline became clearer still.

It was a giant wolf, it stood at least nine feet tall. Its head was lowered between its shoulders and it was sniffing the air as it walked.

Tom looked around in fear for any way of escaping. The surrounding wolves were close, but there was just a chance perhaps if he was fast enough. There was no time to think about it.

Tom suddenly drew his sword with a flash of sparks and light. He dashed off to the side between two trees, his black cloak billowing out behind him. A wolf leapt up at him from the side and Tom struck out with his sword. The blade hit a low pine branch, scattering needles and snow, as Tom veered off in another direction, zigzagging among the trees. Jollity flew off from the branch and flapped about trying to distract the wolves. Tom got as far as a clearing in the trees before the first wolf got its jaws clamped around his boot and brought him down. Tom fell heavily in the snow and lost his grip on his sword. He was flipped over by the wolf which drooled and growled into his face. He felt the other wolves arrive; their cold paws pressed on him and weighed him down. He struggled to sit up but found himself looking straight into a dozen pairs of yellow eyes.

The big wolf howled suddenly and the other wolves dragged Tom back across the snow, pulling him with their jaws. Jollity hovered above them, calling out to Tom, 'Stay calm, Tom, I'll do what I can.'

Tom felt anything but calm. He could feel sharp teeth digging in through his three-and-a-half-league boots. He felt the hard tangled tree roots bumping under him as he was pulled across the snow. The wolves more or less threw him at the feet of the giant wolf.

It finally nuzzled its way between the trees and stood in front of Tom looking down at him.

Its breath was like a fog.

Tom lay very still; he knew there was nothing else he could do. The wolf made a rumbling noise, a growl low in its throat, which set the trees vibrating and more snow falling in clumps from the near branches.

'You walk in my forest without permisson,' the wolf said in its rumbling deep voice.

'I am just a traveller,' Tom stammered out.

'My pack eat any travellers that they find, and they are hungry now.'

'I am on a mission to rescue someone,' Tom said. 'If they were to eat me an innocent will suffer too.'

'No one is innocent,' the giant wolf said, and then growled, 'There isn't much of you but enough to feed some of the cubs perhaps.' The giant wolf breathed in and then a frown crossed its brow, and it breathed in again. The wolf's head came as close to Tom as it could get without actually touching him. The wolf sniffed at him directly and Tom closed his eyes, expecting the worst.

The wolf's huge black nose sniffed and worried at the wolf fur edging of Tom's cloak. The wolf's head pulled back. 'Mmm,' it growled, puzzled, 'you wear the cloak.'

Tom opened his eyes as Jollity landed on the ground among the wolves.

'Hafnir gave him the cloak,' Jollity said brightly.

'Hafnir,' the giant wolf said, turning its huge head towards Jollity. 'Who asked you?'

'No one,' said Jollity, only too aware of the wolves towering over him and surrounding him.

'Let the boy speak,' the wolf said.

'Hafnir did give me the cloak,' Tom said quietly, his eyes closed tight.

'What is your business here?' the wolf said.

'I have come to rescue my father Big Jack Trueheart from the Dark King.'

'Is that all you have come to do?'

'Hafnir said I was the boy in the prophecy.'

'And he gave you this cloak to wear?'

'Yes.'

'A cloak trimmed with fur cut from my own pelt by force.'

'A brave warrior, a hero, did it, he said.'

'I will admit that he was brave and noble,' said the wolf. 'Are you brave?'

'I hope to be,' Tom said, his eyes still tightly closed.

'You mentioned the Dark King; his mischief has already been at work here. You may pass safely on one condition,' the wolf said, in a deep voice like rolling thunder. 'You will put right the wrong that he has done.'

'We'll do our best,' said Tom.

'We?'

'I am his companion and helper,' said Jollity.

The giant wolf looked over at the bird and then down at Tom.

'I hardly believed I would see this day, but it seems to have come true. We must trust our fate to a boy, to this scrawny boy and a crow.'

Jollity flew up into the trees.

Tom opened his eyes, and found himself staring closely into the golden eyes of the giant wolf.

'My pack will guide you safely through the rest of the forest, despite their hunger.'

'Thank you,' Tom managed to stammer out. Jollity flew down and landed on Tom's shoulder.

'Let him up,' the wolf said. The wolves moved away, lifting their paws from Tom, who struggled to his feet. 'Fetch the boy his weapon.'

A wolf brought Tom's sword clamped between its jaws, and dropped it at Tom's feet. Tom sheathed the sword, 'You really are Fenrir then?' Tom said.

'I *am* Fenrir,' the giant wolf said and bowed its head. 'You will need to go much further now, beyond our north lands, if you are to find and destroy the Dark King.'

'We always meant to travel south,' said Tom.

'The south land is divided from the north land by a gigantic wall, as you will find out,' said Fenrir.

They walked on through the trees following Fenrir and his pack of wolves. After half a day of cold silent walking through deep snow they finally reached the edge of the dark forest. The wolves all stopped suddenly and stood in a line well hidden among the trees. The village of white houses was clearly visible now a few leagues away across the plain. The wolves turned as one and set off back into the forest.

'You must leave us here,' said Fenrir, 'your destiny lies that way. Go with the gods, young man.'

'Goodbye,' Tom called to the already retreating wolf pack who were now just blurs of grey.

'They've gone already, Jollity,' he said after a moment's waving at nothing.

Fenrir watched them with his golden eyes from the treeline as they made their way down towards the village.

The village, when they finally reached it, was built next to a lake of almost mirror-like black ice. A few burned-up and blackened skeletons of wooden fishing boats were lined on the shore at a natural inlet. Beyond stood the little village of white houses. They looked as if they had all been burned from above. The roof beams were clearly visible, like blackened bones peeping through the patches of burned thatch or tiles. Black smoke still drifted around the houses. A few of the houses were completely destroyed, flattened against the ground as if by some giant foot. A terrible smell hung over the village: the suffocating stench of sulphur. There was not a single person to be seen. Tom walked into the main street. A cart was turned over in the roadway surrounded by its cargo of rotten vegetables; a few fat black flies hovered over the stinking pulp, otherwise there was nothing moving at all but the drifting smoke.

Then Tom saw that a man sat guard outside one of the houses. His clothes were scorched and ragged as if he had just escaped from a terrible fire. He stood up as Tom and Jollity approached him, and snatched up a huge axe from the ground beside him. The man held the axe up high above his head and moved threateningly towards Tom.

'You stay back, young master,' he called out. 'Go on your way, we want no more strangers here.'

'I am sorry, sir,' said Tom stopping in his tracks. 'You seem to have suffered a tragic accident here.'

'This was no accident,' said the man. 'Visitors came, just like yourself, and then all this happened.'

'Were they pirates then or raiders?' said Tom.

'No, they were no pirates but they might as well

have been. One was a so-called king, and the other was his prisoner. They stole the gold hoard from our dragon.'

'Dragon?' said Tom.

'Yes, our dragon, up in the mountain.' He pointed up to the dark crags above the lake.

'What happened?' said Tom.

'The dragon punished us. It swooped down and burned our village even though we had nothing to do with stealing its hoard. Everyone has fled the place now except me. I am Uhn, called "the watcher", and I must stay.' The man shook his head sadly. 'I have heard the howling of Fenrir and now the winter seems set in for ever. We're done for. It was such a happy village too, such a nice life we had here once on the lake,' he added sadly.

'Where did the king and his prisoner go?'

'Took off up into the sky in their black flying ship just as was prophesied. The dragon chased them. I've not seen them since. The dragon's back though, and surely keeps an eye out now for any strangers. Be off now at once if you value your skin. Clear off as soon as you like,' and he waved his axe threateningly again, 'unless you want to be burned alive.'

Jollity flapped his wings nervously and flew up and then settled back on Tom's other shoulder.

Tom said, 'But you see, that is why we are here. We are looking for that so-called king and his prisoner. We mean to bring him to justice and free the prisoner. When we have done that we shall return here with your dragon's golden hoard, I promise.'

'A word in private, Tom,' said Jollity.

The man suddenly flourished his huge axe. 'That bird, it just spoke to you, yet another creature of ill omen,' he said in shock, and he stepped forward a few paces more towards Tom, waving his axe. 'You are bewitched,' he said, 'an evil pair.' With that he leaped forward and grabbbed Tom around the neck. Jollity flew off in fright. The man held the sharp blade of his double axe head close to Tom's throat. Tom struggled and spoke as best he could with the axe blade so near.

'We mean you no harm, sir, I am Tom Trueheart of the Adventuring Truehearts. We are on a mission to rescue my father Big Jack Trueheart; it was he who was the prisoner of that king, and I can tell you one thing, he's not a real king.'

'Why should I believe anything you say?'

'We are not evil. Tom is indeed a boy of honour, sir,' said Jollity flying back on to Tom's shoulder and fixing the man with his black eyes. 'We were put ashore here by your fellow countryman Hafnir the Bold. He knew of our mission from a prophecy. Why, Fenrir the giant wolf and all his pack just escorted us through the dark forest.'

'Fenrir,' said the man, his eyes widening. 'Fenrir and his pack escorted you here, you say. How big was he, then?'

'As tall as your house and a little more,' said Tom struggling to speak with the axe blade at his throat.

Uhn looked round and his eyes darted wildly, looking at the distant treeline of the forest.

It was then that Fenrir stepped out into the clearing. He sat on his haunches, raised his huge head, and howled into the falling snow.

The man looked terrified.

They all looked across at the huge wolf. Tom waved at Fenrir as if he had just seen one of his best friends.

The wolf stood and nodded back at Tom. It lowered its head in salutation, then it turned and ran back into the forest, kicking up great clumps of snow.

Uhn watched the whole thing in astonishment. He moved the axe blade away from Tom's throat. He lowered the axe with care. Then he leaned on the handle and looked at Tom in fear.

'I am sure that Tom will do his best to fulfil his promise to return your dragon's gold,' said Jollity into the silence.

Tom took a step or two back away from Uhn and his dangerous axe.

'All this ruination was my fault,' said Uhn miserably. 'If I hadn't opened my door that morning and offered shelter to that rotten king and his poor prisoner and told them about our dragon none of this would have happened.'

'You should not blame yourself,' said Tom. 'Did the prisoner say anything to you?'

'Not that I recall,' said Uhn. 'He ate my alebrod, and then they went off and stole the gold. No, wait, there was something. I found this in the empty alebrod bowl after they left.' Uhn rummaged in his pocket and pulled out a little square of cloth, and handed it to Tom.

It was grubby and white with a pattern of red hearts.

'You see,' said Tom, 'it matches the cloth on my pack-staff.'

'Why so it does,' said Uhn. 'Why, if it matches, then that must mean that you are in league with that villain and his henchman.' And Uhn raised his sharp axe again.

'No, sir, I promise,' said Tom, 'that is the pattern of my family the Truehearts. We are the enemy of that so-called king, believe me.'

At that point there came a sudden roaring noise from above. Then there was a bloodcurdling high shrieking, along with sharp leathery cracks and a flapping sound. Uhn looked up, shielding his eyes. 'Oh no no, too late.' He flung himself down onto the blackened snow and the filthy scorched ground, and covered his head with his arms.

'I think you'd better run, boy,' he mumbled from the dirt. 'Hide yourself. Just go. Here comes our dragon, and it is very, very angry.'

Chapter 11

Rumpelstiltskin stopped, exhausted already. Oh, he thought, why wasn't there a nice peasant wood-cutter with a good strong back to ride around on when you needed one? The fierce sunlight dappled the ground at his feet. Since the airship had made its forced landing near the wall he had just managed to keep pace with the striding figures walking ahead of him.

He sighed, took a heavy, damp, goatskin sack from his shoulder and drank some of the cool water from inside. He sat down under the branches of an olive tree. He could see Ormestone and Big Jack Trueheart still on the dusty white road ahead of him. The road snaked around the mountain. The black airship was still visible somewhere above him all tangled up and anchored in a grove of trees directly below the summit of the huge stone dividing wall. The others were halfway down the mountain now and getting away from him. Soon he would have to act. He swigged some more water, stoppered the sack and scanned the road below. As he looked down at the next layer of hot roadway below him something caught his eye. It flashed in the raw sunlight. He scuttled forward to see what it was. Under a coarse prickly bush there was an abandoned warrior's shield made of smooth shiny metal.

'This could be just the thing,' he said out loud to himself. He wanted to be discovered accidentally on the road. Ormestone after all had no idea that his former sprite had hitched a ride on the airship after the fatal battle in the Land of Dark Stories.

He forced himself to crawl under the prickly bush.

He lifted out the shield, which curved outwards. He put the curved side down against the ground, hoisted himself and his water bag into the middle of the shield and kicked away with his left foot. The shield slid forward fast over the hard, hot, scented grass. Shield and sprite tobogganed down the thyme-scented hill-side and slithered to a halt on the next lower twist of the white roadway. Rumpelstiltskin clambered off the shield and brushed himself down. He pitched the shield under another prickly bush at the side of the road and waited for the lean figure of Ormestone and his captive to come round the curve of the hillside.

There was little shade anywhere, just the sparse branches of an olive tree. He stood under the silver leaves and waited, hunched over and hidden, feeling very hot in his thick wintry clothes. He already missed the cold pine forests and the frozen air of the northern half of the Land of Myths and Legends. He was uncomfortably hot and it was still early in the morning.

He did not have to wait long for Ormestone and Jack Trueheart to appear.

The tall figures soon turned the bend in the road, and walked towards him. Ormestone, in his shabby black cloak, led the way, kicking up clouds of white dust with his seven-league boots. Jack Trueheart stumbled along behind him dragging the big sack of stolen sprite gold. A long chain linked the two figures together. Rumpeltstiltskin suddenly stepped out on to the road from behind the tree and stood in front of them.

'Well, well,' Ormestone said, stopping in his tracks, and causing Big Jack Trueheart to stumble into him. 'It's you. I thought we had lost you for good back there hundreds of miles away, days ago.' Ormestone waved his hand vaguely in the direction of the Land of Dark Stories.

'Surely you mean centuries ago, my master,' said Rumpelstiltskin with a smile, bowing low.

'What do you mean, centuries ago?' said Ormestone.

'Why, master, when we crossed the boundary sea we entered another time zone,' said Rumpelstiltskin. 'We have travelled to the Land of Myths and Legends and so we have also travelled back down the years, as well as in distance.'

'Of course we have,' said Ormestone, blustering, 'I knew that.'

Rumpeltstiltskin bowed again. Jack Trueheart said nothing, he just stared at his boots and shook his head; he had after all been to this place before.

'Well,' said Ormestone, 'what do you have to say for yourself, and why are you here?'

'I am sorry, master, your highness, but I was wrong to harbour any anger towards you about what happened with the princesses back there in the Land of Dark Stories. I came here to apologize and humbly offer all my services to you again, should you need them.'

'I see,' Ormestone said. He thought fast, this was better than he could have hoped. 'I am sure to need some sprite magic too at some point,' he added almost casually.

Rumpelstiltskin doffed his hat so that it scraped on the hot dusty road. 'So it shall be, your highness.'

'This is, I believe, a place of fundamentals,' said Ormestone, 'a place of elemental forces, a place of extremes of heat and cold, a place of ancient stories. The birthplace of the deepest and darkest of all stories. They will suit my purposes very well. You say we are back in time, well then, we can affect the very future of all stories at their root. There will be no limits to what we might achieve here?'

'All true, your majesty, but there are limits to my own abilities,' the little sprite said.

'I repeat, there will be no limits here,' said Ormestone, spreading his arms wide and staring wildly down at Rumpelstiltskin.

'Very well, of course, master, I will do my best.' Inside, Rumpelstiltskin seethed with his own plans for Ormestone's destruction, and how he could get to see his lovely princesses again. None of this was to be admitted to anyone, of course. He smiled back at Ormestone who trudged off while Rumpelstiltskin kept up at his side.

Poor Jack Trueheart, chained and awkward, stumbled along behind them. He looked as if all the trouble of the world were on his shoulders, not just a heavy sack of sprite gold. He stared at the ground for any chance or place to leave another clue to whoever he hoped might be following after them. He stopped in his tracks, put the sack of gold down on the path, and sat on it heavily. This pulled Ormestone up short. He turned and walked over to Jack.

'Well?' he said, tapping his boot impatiently on the road.

'Sorry, your majesty, but I need a drink of water.'

'Feeble, like all you so-called adventurers.'

'Allow me, master,' Rumpelstiltskin said, scuttling forward with his sack of water. He unstoppered it and Jack drank gratefully from it, allowing some of the water to dribble from his mouth on to the dry ground.

'Don't waste it,' Ormestone snapped.

The water made a little muddy patch on the road, and Big Jack let one of the gold coins he had managed to snag from inside his sack drop down into the mud, then he stood up and hefted the sack back up to his shoulder, and they all set off once more.

The little coin sat in the wet earth. Soon the water would dry out in the heat, sealing the coin in edge upwards, just as Jack had hoped. It would sit there golden and winking in the bright light just calling out to be noticed.

Chapter 12

A MEETING WITH A DRAGON

9.03 A.M.

Tom looked up. He saw the dragon circling above them. Jollity flew off his shoulder and flew round Tom but kept his distance from the dragon. Uhn lay just where he was, not even daring to look up at the monster. Tom could see that there was nowhere to hide. All the village houses, including Uhn's, were after all not much more than charred ruins, open to the cold sky. The dragon landed, flexed its huge wings, threw its head back and roared out a burst of bright flame. Then it lowered its head and walked forward towards Tom and Uhn. It had been watching for any sign of a visitor, any stranger like the ones that stole its hoard, and as soon as Tom had appeared it had set off ready for vengeance.

The dragon made a noise halfway between a growl and a roar. It made the earth quiver and rock beneath their feet. Tom thought that the giant wolf Fenrir had been bad enough but this was on another scale altogether. He stared straight ahead at the creature. He had never seen anything like it. Little puffs of smoke drifted from its nostrils and there was a strong hot smell of sulphur.

Tom took one step forward towards the monster, his hand on his sword hilt.

'I am very sorry,' he said nervously, hoping that the dragon might understand him, 'but I did not take your gold.'

The dragon tilted its head on one side, opened its mouth, and blew a searing little jet of flame so that Tom was forced to step backwards.

'I know who took it and I will find the person that stole your hoard of gold,' said Tom more nervously, 'and I will bring it all back to you, every piece, I promise.'

The dragon blew a longer, brighter burst of flame

towards them causing a nearby thorn bush to burst into flame.

'It's no good,' said Uhn, mumbling against the ground, 'you can't reason with a dragon.'

Jollity swooped down and flew towards the dragon.

'No,' Tom called out, 'Jollity, don't.' The dragon roared and then lowered its head to improve its aim. It shot another burst of heat and sulphur out towards Tom, and Tom was forced down against the ground too, alongside Uhn. He pulled his sword slowly out of the scabbard. He held it out along the ground in front of him.

Jollity the crow flew straight towards the dragon and tried to land on its shining snout. The dragon raised its head high and loosed another burst of flame and black smoke straight at the bird.

The smoke thickened around Jollity, and Tom couldn't see what had happened to him. He leapt to his feet and called out, 'Jollity!' He held his sword high and it sparked brightly in the drifting smoke. Another huge bolt of flame shot just past Tom, scorching the back of his jerkin. He felt a sensation of terrible heat and he could scarcely breathe in the sulphurous smoke.

One more blast of those flames and fireballs, he thought, and it would all be over before it had begun. Tom threw himself down again and rolled across the cold ground. Jollity was staggering about in the dirty snow, shaking soot from his feathers.

'Are you all right?' Tom shouted.

'A bit scorched, Tom; I'll live,' Jollity called back.

The bird lifted off the ground again and Tom watched in horror as Jollity flew straight at the dragon. As the bird flew it called out something; Tom could not understand what Jollity had said.

The dragon tilted its head on one side and its eyes widened as Jollity landed close by. The dragon stopped blowing fireballs and seemed to listen to what Jollity was saying. After a few seconds Jollity flew over and landed on Tom's shoulder.

'Well,' said Jollity, 'I told her about us and your promise.'

The dragon shuffled closer to them on its clawed feet, smoke billowing from its nostrils.

Uhn called out, 'This is it, we're all doomed now,' and he buried his face back under his arms.

'Her?' said Tom.

'Yes,' said Jollity, 'she is a proud lady dragon.'

'I didn't know you could speak dragon,' said Tom.

'You never asked me, Tom,' said Jollity.

The dragon was close enough to smell now. Close enough too for Tom to feel the heat from inside it, and smell the sulphur and the brimstone, and the hot leathery hide which was a bright green colour.

Jollity stepped forward towards the dragon, and spoke some more. The dragon lowered its head, tilted it on one side, then replied to Jollity in low rumblings.

Jollity said, 'I explained our mission. She has offered to fly you as far as the border wall with the south.'

Tom looked up at the dragon; it stared back at him with its great glassy eyes; a smudge of black smoke emerged from its nostrils.

'That was where Ormestone's airship went,' Jollity went on. 'She cannot cross over the border wall, that will be as far as she can take us.'

'You mean I have to ride on that thing?'

'Yes, Tom, you do.'

'Did you tell her that we would bring back her hoard?' said Tom.

Jollity spoke again; the dragon replied and then lifted its head and roared out a huge ball of flame into the cold air.

'To be honest, she insists on it,' said Jollity.

Uhn stood up slowly and stepped carefully away from them shaking his head. 'You are both bewitched,' he said. He kept his distance from the dragon and retreated, walking behind his axe, back to the shelter of his ruined doorway. He sat on the step of his burned house.

Tom called over to him, 'We will return the gold and then you will be able to rebuild your village.'

'You are a good, well-meaning boy,' said Uhn, 'but

I cannot ever see such a thing happening. Will we really be rebuilding all this soon? Oh, I do hope so,' he said gloomily. 'If you bring back the gold and if this Fimbul of a winter ever clears.'

Jollity said, 'Come on then, Tom, time to go south now.'

Tom was holding the little fragment of Trueheart cloth that Uhn had given him. He rubbed it between his fingers. It was a token at least, a sign left by his father that they were following the right trail.

Tom didn't much like the idea of going even closer to the dragon. It was a fearsome looking thing. He could feel the heat inside it even from where he stood. It smelled too, of sulphur and chemicals, and its big gold-green eyes glared at him. How was Tom to know that it was not about to engulf him in a great fireball? He hesitated, all his recent bravery suddenly gone. Climbing on to Jollity the crow's back when Tom was the size of a thumb had been one thing, Jollity was his friend, after all, and soft and feathery. But climbing on to the back of something so full of heat and danger, something so heavily armoured and spiky was another thing altogether. Tom didn't want to do it. Jollity flew over and landed on his shoulder.

'What's the matter, Tom?' he said.

'I think that the dragon is too big and too frightening to sit on,' Tom whispered.

'She's really very nice,' said Jollity, 'I've been talking to her.'

'I noticed,' said Tom.

'Come on now, climb on her back,' said Jollity. 'She is impatient for us to be off in pursuit of her missing hoard.'

Tom tucked the little square of faded Trueheart cloth into his travel bag, picked up his packstaff, and walked closer to the dragon. Jollity lifted from his shoulder and circled above him. Tom waved to Uhn. 'We will be back with the hoard,' he called out.

'It'll be a long, long, long, terrible winter, young master, if you don't,' Uhn replied, shaking his head.

Jollity landed on the dragon's back.

'Climb up, Tom, come on now, don't worry,' the crow said.

Tom tucked his packstaff into his belt, reached up and held on to one of the horned spikes which ran along the ridges and seams of the dragon's armour-plated green hide. He pulled himself up on to the body of the dragon. He could feel the glow of heat inside the belly. It was not unpleasant; it was a bit like sitting slightly too near the fire on a winter's day back at home. He made his way carfully across the creature's back past another row of spikes and settled himself, just as he had done on Jollity, on the ridge just forward of the wings.

Jollity said something to the dragon and then flew off. The dragon's wings lifted and fell. The dragon stood and raised its long neck. Then it ran forward, thumping past the burned village. Its wings flapped faster and faster, and then suddenly it eased off the ground and soared up into the cold sky. This was nothing like flying on Jollity's back. The dragon was very fast. Tom could feel his skin stretching back on his face. The upper air was icy, but luckily the dragon was heated from within and so Tom didn't feel the cold much at all.

The great dark-green forest stretched below them for miles. If Tom turned his head and looked behind he could see the fjords and the cold grey ocean, topped with white foam riders. He even thought he could see Hafnir's ship proudly bobbing on the waves. He couldn't be sure, but he waved anyway in case they were watching. Jollity flew close by alongside and they ploughed on fast through the scattered snow showers and heavy grey skies.

Many hours of very fast flying were ahead during which Tom curled up against the heat of the dragon and napped.

When Tom woke up he saw something huge looming up on the horizon ahead. It stretched from one side of the island to the other, right across the land. It rose up seemingly hundreds of feet into the air. As they flew closer Tom saw that it was a wall. An enormous wall, made up of great oblong blocks of rough stone stacked up high into the air. It was an ancient wall; even from miles away Tom could see that the stone was pitted, and covered over with great green patches of moss and lichen. Jollity, who had been hitching a lift on the dragon's tail, settled suddenly on Tom's shoulder.

'That's the wall that divides the land. Once beyond it we shall enter the southern half of the Land of Myths and Legends. Our dragon cannot cross over. We will have to make our way across without her help.'

The dragon took a while to slow down. It circled lower and lower while the wall loomed higher and higher above them. The top of the wall was shrouded in a cold looking fog and Tom could see nothing of the land on the other side.

The dragon landed on a patch of scrubland a few hundred yards or so from the terrifying wall. The wall was at least as high as the dark castle in the Land of Dark Stories, perhaps even higher. When Tom looked up at it, it almost looked as if the wall were about to fall down on top of him. It made Tom shiver and feel queasy. He felt just as he had when he had to think of going up the huge beanstalk back in the Land of Stories.

He climbed carefully down from the dragon's warm back. Jollity flew down and landed near the dragon's head. Tom walked bravely over and stood near the snout. He could see the bright teeth showing and the little curls of green smoke drifting out of the creature's nostrils.

'Thank you for that ride,' Tom said.

Jollity translated Tom's words; well, the crow made some noises, in any case, and the dragon nodded her head in response.

'I shall make sure that I bring all your lost hoard of gold back to you, I promise,' Tom added.

Jollity made some more odd noises to the dragon and then the dragon responded. She made some low grunting noises deep in her belly, and then she lifted her head high and let out a great bright orange and yellow fireball into the air. Tom could feel the great heat of it as it flowed up into the snowflakes. The dragon lowered its head and pointed its snout forwards. A little clump of pine trees was growing on the lower slopes of land next to the huge wall. Their dark branches and clumps of dark green needles shadowed the stone. The dragon let loose another fireball straight at the trees. The trees burst into flame, and the dragon roared and turned, flapped its wings and rose above them as the trees burned. It set off back where it had come from, flying fast and letting out more bursts of flame. Tom waved up at the dragon as she flew away. 'Goodbye,' he called out. 'You'll get your gold back.'

117

'She understands, Tom, and she will be waiting. So for poor old Uhn's sake let's hope we can deliver that gold.'

'I wonder why she burned those trees?' Tom said.

The trees were blazing fiercely, and a pall of dark smoke drifted up the face of the wall. One of the trees suddenly fell against the others with a crash. Jollity said, 'She seemed to do it so deliberately, it was just like that archer who fired the flaming arrow to show us the way. Mm, I wonder?' He flew over and hovered above the smoke. He flew back and settled on Tom's shoulder. 'Let's just wait for the fire to burn out.' Tom walked closer to the wall. He could feel the warmth from the burning trees, and smelt that familiar smell, woodsmoke scented with resin, like the cosy fires at home, and he wondered for a moment how everyone was doing after the big wedding. He imagined that they were all on the Island of Happy Ever After by now.

And then he remembered.

He was back somewhere in time. Where he was now there were no brothers yet, no cosy home, nothing of his past life. He was beyond the boundary

sea; that was all to come. It made him shiver; he had
goosepimples just imagining such a thing. He stepped
closer to the fire and held his hands out to warm
them.

He looked into the dwindling flames. Dragon's fire
certainly consumed things quickly. The trees were very
nearly hot white ash already. He walked a little closer.

'Careful, Tom,' Jollity said.

'Just keeping warm,' Tom said, holding his hands
out towards the scented wood ash. It was then that
Tom, looking at the wall behind the smouldering trees,
noticed that there was a huge bronze door.

Part Two
In A Hot Place

Chapter 13

THE BRONZE DOOR

7.37 P.M.

Tom waited for the burning trees to dwindle down to nothing. He impatiently cleared the smouldering ash away with the end of his packstaff. He made a path through the hot ash up to the huge dark door. Jollity flew over and perched on the top of the door frame.

'I thought so,' Jollity said. 'The dragon has brought us straight to one of the doors in the wall that lead through to the south side. It's easy for me, I can fly over and land on the other side, but it's a bit high and dangerous as a climb for you. There are some tree branches and vines, now I look, but your only sensible choice would be to use the door here.'

Tom stepped right up to the door. It towered above him, a great solid slab of heavy bronze with huge ornate hinges, and a covered lock. Tom slid the lock cover aside. He stood on tiptoes and put his eye to the keyhole. He looked through. He could see nothing. There was just a solid wall of darkness. There was no sign of a land beyond the door. He pushed against it. It didn't move.

'Its locked,' he said. He kicked at the door with his boot and it made a dull metallic ringing noise, a deep bell note.

'It'll be hard to force a door this big,' he said to Jollity. Then he had a thought. He looked around for any fragments of metal. There was nothing at all, only stems and twigs and blackened wood and ash. He unwrapped his packstaff and poked about among his stuff.

'Ah,' he said, 'this might do the trick. Jacques once picked a lock and opened a door without a key, I remember. He just twisted something like this in the lock.' Tom held up the little metal opener he sometimes had to use to prise the lids and stoppers off his mother's ginger beer bottles.

He piled up some branches and old logs and stood

as high as he could, and reached the little opener into the bronze lock. He poked around in the inside of the lock. He had no idea what he was doing. He could feel bits of mechanism, he touched things and twisted things and pressed things, but the lock remained firmly locked.

Tom had something to eat and then tried again. Jollity watched him. 'Quite a trick to picking a lock, Tom.'

'I can see that,' said Tom. 'Oh, where's Jacques when you need him?'

'A long way away, I'm afraid, Tom,' said Jollity.

'Looks like I might be trapped here in the Norse Lands after all.' Tom turned to face his old friend. 'The only other way is up.' He pointed to the top of the towering wall. 'And that looks very very high, higher even than the old beanstalk.'

'Well, you managed to climb that, with a little help,' Jollity said. 'I'll fly up to the top and see what's what,' the bird added.

The crow took off at once and spiralled upwards. Tom watched him grow smaller and smaller as he neared the top of the wall. It was certainly a long climb, but as he looked he could see that it really was not much worse than the beanstalk which he had already climbed a few short months ago. And if he could do that then he should certainly be able to climb this now.

Jollity flew back down and settled above the bronze door.

'Well, it's quite a climb, Tom, but I think you can do it.'

'I know I can do it,' said Tom standing up straight and as tall as he could. He picked up his packstaff, tucked it into his belt, checked his sword, and then set off to climb the wall.

He could not tell exactly how high the wall was but it was certainly hundreds of feet. There were deep cracks and fissures in the pitted and weathered stone. The blocks were so big that there was enough of a gap between them for him to fit his boots into comfortably. It was like climbing a very shallow vertical staircase. He was able to make slow and steady progress. Jollity hovered near him, from time to time encouraging him.

'What mustn't you do, Tom?'

'Look down,' said Tom.

'Exactly,' said Jollity.

The blocks of stone got smaller towards the top of the wall. Climbing was suddenly more difficult. Luckily there were some vines and creepers growing and spilling over from the top of the wall. Tom held on to them and used them to get himself up the last few feet.

He finally pulled himself up on to the top of the wall in a cloud of cold mist. He was able to stand comfortably, for the top of the wall, or what little he could see of it, seemed wide. He walked very carefully from his side of the wall to the other. He emerged suddenly from the swirling cloud of grey winter mist into blazing sunlight and summer heat.

He stood for a moment and looked at the astonishing view laid out below him. A great green sunny landscape stretched all the way to a distant blue sea. The dividing line between the sea and the sky was hard to see, because both were of an almost equal and intense blue. He breathed in, and the air seemed to be scented with thyme and other pungent herbs, and he had never felt so fiercely warm before.

The wall was built on a sloping hillside. The grass below looked almost golden, sun-baked and dry. There was a stand of tall dark-green cypress trees below the wall and silvery green olive groves stretched away down the hillside beside a curving white road. White buildings dotted the landscape and he could even see some statues among the trees.

Directly below him the wall stretched dizzyingly smooth down into the bright sunlight. This side of the wall was made of a bright white marble veined with fine grey lines. It appeared to be one sheer slab of stone, no cracks or fissures, no joins, no footholds at all. He had forgotten one simple thing on his way up. He was going to have to get all the way down again. He could see no way of doing that.

Somewhere among the sunlight and shadow and the cypress trees directly below him he could see a small white building with steps and a row of columns. Beside the building he could see a large softly rounded black shape billowing in the wind and tucked almost hidden among the trees. It looked familiar. The sunlight was so hot that Tom took the wolf fur cape from around his shoulders and tucked it into his packstaff bundle. Jollity flew over and settled on his shoulder.

'You see, Tom,' Jollity said, 'you did it, climbed up all this way. Quite a big view, eh?'

'Oh it's a big view, all right,' Tom said, 'but I need to get down there, and it's a long way down, and there are no footholds at all.'

'Do you see that black shape down there; I think that's Ormestone's air machine. Wait here, Tom,' Jollity said, and the crow flew off.

He watched the bird getting smaller and smaller as it spiralled away down the sheer cliff face of marble wall.

As Tom looked down his head began to spin. Whether it was the sudden heat after the cold, or just the giddy height of the wall, Tom felt dizzy. He swayed where he stood and his eyes could hardly focus, everything seemed so far away. He put his hand out to steady himself and felt his boot slip against the smooth marble. He heard a sudden shout from Jollity, as the bird flew back up. 'No, Tom!' But it was too late, Tom simply fell right off the top of the wall and Jollity could do nothing to save him.

Chapter 14

A NEW STORY

SOME DAYS EARLIER. LATE AFTERNOON

Ormestone, Big Jack, and Rumpelstiltskin made a strange sight on the roads of the ancient land. Jack was bent over with the heavy sack of gold on his strong back, and, of course, he was joined to Ormestone by the sprite chain. Rumpelstiltskin looked hot and uncomfortable trudging along in his winter clothes, with all the while a dark bubble of secret bitterness welling up inside him. Only Ormestone looked content, even happy. Here he was in the birthplace of stories, the cradle of tales. Here was his chance to influence every story told for ever in the future. His chance at last to really shut down even the slight possibility of a

131

happy ending to any story ever, starting right now. Also, of course, his chance to find and plunder even more beautiful gold than the dragon's hoard.

He marched ahead of the other two, his usual black cloak tucked away, his white shirt rippling in the warm winds, his big boots kicking up clouds of white dust. Every so often Big Jack did his best to let slip one of the smaller gold coins onto the roadway. They travelled downhill during the long afternoon and soon they were in sight of the sea and a fine city of white marble.

There was an inn on the edge of the city. A modest building made of timber with a stable block and a thatched roof. It nestled under a grove of trees which shaded the gardens and kept everything nice and cool in the courtyard. There was a fountain and a fine marble statue of a goddess. Ormestone strode into the garden and a servant in a short tunic hurried up to him.

'A flagon of your finest wine for us, and some water for my prisoner here,' Ormestone said, 'and send the landlord to me.'

'Yes, sire,' the servant said and hurried off into the inn.

Ormestone sat at one of the outdoor tables. Jack put

the sack of gold down and sat heavily on the edge of the fountain and cooled himself. Rumpelstiltskin took in the surroundings, the statue of a fair goddess, the prospect of the sea, the fine quality of the buildings beyond the inn. A rich city, he thought.

The landlord hurried out, and looked over his oddly dressed visitors. There was something of the brigand or pirate about them, something very worrying to a native of their city.

'Good day, gentlemen,' he said warily.

'Good day, my man,' said Ormestone. 'A meal, if you please, landlord, and no porridge with snails,' he added, shuddering at the memory of the awful alebrod.

'No indeed, sir,' the landlord replied. He paused and looked down at Ormestone's dusty boots, and then at the shabby tall man sitting by the fountain chained to him, and finally at little Rumpelstiltskin in his dark clothes with a trophy of oak leaves wrapped about his head.

Ormestone plunged his hand into the sack and pulled out a handful of the gold hoard coins.

At that moment the stitched-faced man arrived at the inn. He had been following them along the road and he came and stood next to Ormestone, towering over the landlord.

'My credit is good, as you can plainly see,' said Ormestone, indicating the gold coins, and then he gestured up to the stitched-faced man just to show that if necessary he had muscle as well as money. 'Have no fear of us, my man, you will be paid, and paid well. Now snap to it.'

The landlord clapped his hands as he raced back inside the inn. They heard him shouting orders.

'This is a rich city, master,' said Rumpelstiltskin, nodding his head.

'Don't think I haven't noticed,' said Ormestone. 'There will be gold and more here, I sense it.'

They ate a feast. Ormestone was in a generous mood, and even Big Jack Trueheart was given plenty of scraps from the table, as if he were Ormestone's favourite dog.

Within a day, using unlimited credit on only the *promise* of his wealth from the dragon's hoard, Ormestone had established himself in a furnished marble villa, close to

the old king's palace and with a fine terrace view of
the harbour and the glorious sea.

Big Jack was locked in the cellar at the villa under
the stern eyes of the stitched-faced man.

It was not long before a messenger arrived at the door
of the villa inviting Ormestone and Rumpelstiltskin to
a special meeting of the citizens and elders at a party
to be held in the nearby royal palace.

Big Jack was left behind under guard, chained in his
secure basement chamber. The walls of the cellar were
lined with old jars and flagons, and even some chem-
ical retorts. Whoever had lived in the villa before
seemed to have had an interest in the natural sciences.
Jack went around the room as far as the sprite chain
would allow studying the labels on each jar with great
interest.

Ormestone and Rumpelstiltskin stood out oddly in
their northern climate clothes among the city's worthies
and elders in their tunics, and yet no one seemed to

notice or mind their appearance. The group of citizens were on the whole a preoccupied and sad looking lot. One of them stepped forward, bowed low, and introduced himself.

'Forgive me, sire,' he said, 'my name is Daedalus, and may I bid you welcome to our kingdom.' The man continued brightly, 'Our people have noticed your arrival. They have remarked, forgive me, that you have something of a fine and regal look about you.'

'How observant and wise those people are, for I am indeed that noblest of things . . . a king,' said Ormestone, standing as straight and proud as he could. 'I am from another country far from here. I am at present in . . . er . . . voluntary exile.'

'You see, sire, it is this way; our own king has long vanished,' Daedalus said. 'He was unable to withstand the pirates that raid us continually, and also the terrible curse, a certain thing, which he had me secure for him on the island you can see over there.'

'A terrible curse, a *thing*?' said Ormestone, immediately interested.

Another citizen stepped forward quickly. 'Come now, Daedalus, enough of that gloomy talk, you will frighten our honoured guests with your nonsense. I am Adelphos, captain of the guard.' The figure bowed from the waist. 'What my friend is trying to say, sire, is that we really are in dire need of a king. Indeed, we were only recently discussing the idea of electing a new kind of leader from among our worthy citizens, but then you arrived and I think you may be in need of a kingdom?'

'A kingdom? Why yes indeed,' Ormestone said.

Rumpelstiltskin tugged at his sleeve but Ormestone ignored him. 'I am used to ruling a kingdom and do feel that need badly, I will admit.'

'Good, good,' said Adelphos, 'this is all better than we could have hoped.'

'I presume,' said Ormestone, 'that I may issue decrees and so forth, engage in profitable wars, instigate gold mining, all that sort of thing?'

Adelphos appeared to hesitate for just a moment. 'Of course, sire, but there will be no need for any gold mining, for the treasury has plenty of gold already.'

'I can never surround myself with enough gold,' said Ormestone.

'Fellow elders, citizens,' Adelphos called out, 'I am happy to announce that our distinguished visitor has agreed to our request. We have indeed found ourselves a new ruler, a new king. It has been a long wait.' Adelphos raised Ormestone's arm; there was a scattering of applause from the elders.

Rumpelstiltskin pulled Daedalus aside while the crowd applauded. They went outside together on to the terrace which overlooked the sea.

'Carry on with what you were saying just now about this terrible thing,' Rumpelstiltskin said, 'it was most interesting to me, if troubling.'

'Yes,' said Daedalus, 'our kingdom is cursed.'

'Cursed,' said Rumpelstiltskin, 'how so?'

'Yes, cursed. I fear your master may have grasped a poisoned chalice.'

'Explain,' said Rumpelstiltskin.

Daedalus pointed over the sea to the dark island some way off the coast.

'Some years ago now,' he said, 'we fought constant battles with a distant king from over there. Eventually our king made a bargain with the distant king to keep the peace. Every nine years we would allow six of our young men and six of our young women to be sacrificed to a terrible monster, the Minotaur, half man and half bull, born in shame to their queen. I myself built the labyrinth maze on the island where the monster lives still, exacting its toll.'

'Is that why you need a new king?' Rumplestiltskin asked.

'Yes, our old king could not live with the shame of his bargain and the hatred of the people. He fled some while ago.'

'When is the next sacrifice due?'

'Soon, I fear. Perhaps our new king will find a way to end the bargain with honour?'

* * *

Later, back at the villa, Ormestone took most of the dragon's hoard from the sack and spilled it out like a golden blanket all across his bed. And then he lay down on the gold and he laughed and kicked and rolled about among all the hundreds of coins. Rumpelstiltskin shook his head.

'Now I have a new kingdom,' Ormestone said, and a great yellow-toothed smile spread across his narrow face.

'About this kingdom, sire,' Rumpelstiltskin began.

'Let me correct you at once; I am no longer simply "sire", I am, once again, "your majesty".'

'Apologies, your majesty.' Rumpelstiltskin bowed low. 'One of the citizens has told me something about this kingdom, something you really should know. Something dark and threatening but also something which I think you will like.'

'Stop faffing about, man, and tell me then, at once,' Ormestone said, sitting up and allowing a cascade of golden coins to spill through his fingers.

Rumpelstiltskin took a deep breath, and began to tell Ormestone the story that Daedalus had just told him.

* * *

The next morning Ormestone, his head full of new schemes, went with Rumpelstiltskin and the stitched-faced man to look over the new palace. It had been empty for nine long years after the last king took flight. The building was gloomy, the guards seemed slack and listless. Clearly Ormestone would have to deal with them. He thought that he could rely on Adelphos, his strong captain of the guard, to kick them into shape.

Ormestone took Adelphos with the others and went down at once to the underground palace coffers. This was where all the gold was kept. Through the iron bars of the chamber he could see that there was something chained up down among the shadows. It was something huge, hunched over, and monstrous looking.

'What is that?' he said to Adelphos.

'He guards the gold against pirate raids,' Adelphos replied.

'He looks terrifying.'

'Enough to put off the fiercest pirate, your majesty.'

Ormestone had the gate unlocked and then sent the stitched-faced man ahead of him into the gold chamber. The stitched-faced man held a lamp and crouched through the doorway. Once inside, though, he could stand tall because the curved ceiling was very high. The huge creature, half as high again as a man, was slumped over in the corner shielding its face from the light. The lamp light was reflected on all the golden vessels which had been hidden away for so long. The creature growled. The stitched-faced man somehow calmed it. He made soothing noises and there seemed to be an instant sort of rapport between them.

'An understanding of monsters,' said Ormestone quietly.

Ormestone, Adelphos, and Rumpelstiltskin went in too.

The creature stood up and shuffled itself into the corner.

'What kind of mythical monster is that?' Ormestone asked.

The creature, at the sound of Ormestone's voice, turned its head to face him. It raised its chained hands high above its head and let out a blood-curdling roar.

With the hands now away from its face, Ormestone saw at once exactly what kind of monster it was.

'I have seen the likeness of this creature before on an engraving at the story bureau,' said Rumpelstiltskin. 'An ancient and fearful monster as befits this place.'

'Indeed,' said Ormestone. 'Bring all the gold up to the king's chamber above,' Ormestone said to the guards. 'As for our monstrous friend here, I have a job for him which will bring him out at last into the sunlight and fresh air.'

'A job, master?' said Rumpelstiltskin.

'Oh yes, an important job. What after all do I have to fear in this place?'

Rumpelstiltskin was tempted to offer himself up as an example but held back; his time would come. 'I really don't know, your highness,' he said.

'Why the pursuing Truehearts, of course,' said Ormestone. 'This fine hideous creature will be let loose, under the guard of our stitched-faced friend, of course, who after all seems to have a strong empathy with the creature already. Between them they will set a trap for any little Trueheart fancying himself as a hero that comes here looking for Daddy.'

Chapter 15

FALLING

As Tom fell he was at first only partly conscious of what had just happened to him. The sudden noisy rush of warm air seemed to bring him round. He found himself tumbling head over heels just clear of the sheer white marble wall. He was aware of Jollity flying down beside him. He looked into his old friend's eyes and saw fear and panic written there. He turned over again in the air so that he faced downwards suddenly, and he could clearly see the once far away golden sunlit ground was coming fast, rushing up to meet him. He shouted out in terror but his cry was snatched away by the air.

'Goodbye, Jollity,' he managed to say inside his head, as he fell faster and faster so that it felt as if he were an arrow that had just been fired from a bow. He had never felt anything quite like it before. It was terrifying but it was also, strangely, very, very exciting; and then he blacked out.

The black airship balloon flapped and billowed now in the warm afternoon winds. Its white skull decoration was gleaming and sinister in the bright sunlight. It was still almost fully inflated, days after the crash landing; although the air was gradually seeping out of it.

The curved top of the balloon blimp suddenly fell inwards in a rush as Tom Trueheart crashed into it. There was a great cloud of dust and pollen and a whole flock of bright noisy birds flew up squawking and shrieking among the dark cypress trees. Tom bounced back upwards high into the air and turned head over heels and then fell back again on to the soft air cushion. He bounced up again a little less high and then the balloon fabric seemed to shiver all over and settle back to where it had been before Tom hit it.

Jollity flew down and settled on the skin of the balloon. Tom was sprawled on his back across the black fabric and he was quite still. Jollity walked over and looked at him. Close to he looked as if he were shaking or shivering, his eyes were closed and his packstaff and travel bag were all tangled up around his arms. He suddenly sat up and burst out laughing. 'Ooh,' he said, 'I want to do that again.'

'Again, Tom,' Jollity said in shock, 'you want to do that again? Look up there, look how far you fell. You were very, very lucky. If the balloon hadn't been here I dread to think how you would have ended up. Like one big splat of Mrs Trueheart's home-made strawberry jam, I should think.'

'I didn't though, did I,' Tom said, standing up and wobbling on the balloon. He smiled as he untangled the packstaff and bag from around himself, hobbled across the wobbly surface of the balloon skin, and slid down one of the ropes to the ground.

'You do recognize this thing, don't you, Tom?' said Jollity.

'Oh yes, I recognize it, all right. It just proves we were right to come here all along. I never expected to be saved by Ormestone's air machine of all things. They must be just ahead of us. Come on,' said Tom, 'I have a father to rescue and a villain to stop.' He set off at once down through the grove of cypress trees to the dusty looking white roadway which wound its way around the hill all the way to the valley below.

'Well, I suppose we had better go this way,' said Jollity landing on Tom's shoulder, 'we have little choice.'

Tom stepped out onto the hot roadway. Just where the road started some fine capital letters were cut deeply into the stone. 'ARCADIA,' Tom read out. 'We are in Arcadia,' he added.

'So it seems, Tom,' and Jollity took off at once from Tom's shoulder and flew on ahead. He waited for Tom to catch him up, just as they had done once before on their first long journey through the Land of Stories.

'This is like old times, Tom,' Jollity said.

'Yes,' said Tom, 'except it was never this hot.'

Tom walked the white road keeping his eyes peeled for any sign that Ormestone and Big Jack had passed that way too, but he saw nothing much. The white dust on the road was disturbed anyway, scuffed over and windblown. There were marks that could have been footprints but it was hard to tell. They had a good view over the landscape in any case. Steep hills and mountains spread out below them and somewhere far off in the distance he could see the horizon, a line of crystal blue sea with a dark island just off shore. It was a very beautiful place, but very different to the northern side. This Arcadia was warm and smelled of flowers and herbs. Parts of the ground on either side of the road were covered over in brightly coloured clumps of wild flowers like a patterened carpet.

Jollity suddenly flew close calling out, 'Stop, Tom, don't move.'

Tom hesitated with one foot held awkwardly in the air just above the road.

'Just below your foot, Tom, look.'

Tom stepped back and looked down. There was a

little mound of earth sticking up from the road and in the middle of it something glinted in the light. Tom bent forward and picked a gold coin out from the dried mud. Jollity landed on his shoulder. Tom held the coin out on his palm. It was heavy and slightly irregular in shape. It had a dragon picked out in relief on one side, and on the other a series of strange letter shapes.

'Runes,' said Jollity.

'Runes?' said Tom puzzled.

'Runes are the letters used in the northern lands where we just were. This is surely one of the stolen coins from that dragon's hoard, Tom.'

Tom put the coin carefully into his travel bag. 'Dropped here, perhaps on purpose to show us the way,' he said. 'In any case, one down, the rest of the hoard to go.'

'It's getting dark, I can sense the shadows creeping in,' Jollity said, 'we'd better find somewhere to sleep.'

Tom and Jollity settled for the night in a cool grove of

oak trees, near the statue of a girl. Nightingales sang sweetly around them in the trees.

'This place is very beautiful,' Tom said. 'It looks beautiful, and it smells beautiful, and it even sounds beautiful; listen to those birds.'

'Nightingales they are called, Tom. We have them in the south of the Land of Stories as well, you just don't hear them so often.'

'I wonder what Ormestone will try to do here?' Tom said.

'I fear he will try and take revenge on you all,' Jollity said.

'How could he do that? My brothers are away by now, safe on the Isle of Happy Ever After.'

'True,' said Jollity, 'but he has your father in his clutches, Tom, and you are here now. He could hurt both of you and that would be bad enough.'

'How do the stories work here?' Tom asked.

'I have no idea, Tom, this is my first visit too. I know that they have oracles and soothsayers and terrifying mythic beasts of all kinds and that stories are told not written. At least, I think that is how it works. They have heroes too.'

'Perhaps I could be a hero,' Tom said brightly.

'Oh, I think you are already that,' Jollity said, 'that's what worries me.'

In the morning after a long walk Tom sat by the road on a green tussock. He delved into his packstaff bundle. The tangled grasses underfoot gave off the strong heady scents of herbs, which had made Tom feel hungry. Jollity flew down. 'Nothing to eat in here,' Tom said, shaking his curly head. 'We have now collected all these coins though from the dragon's hoard, ten in all. I am guessing Big Jack dropped them for us to find.'

'I am sure he did,' Jollity said. 'There is a town a little further down the road. You might find a tavern and something to eat there; you could buy a lot of breakfast with one of those coins.'

'Can't use those,' said Tom, 'I'll have to find another way to pay.'

Further on down the path Tom saw a shepherd sitting in the shade with his flock and playing a sweet tune on his pipes. He waved to Tom as he passed by and called out, 'Break bread with me, young traveller.'

Tom walked up the hillside a little way away from the path. Jollity flew after him and settled on the tree.

'I am Dorcon,' the shepherd said.

'I am Tom, and this is my companion Jollity,' Tom said pointing up to the crow in the tree.

'Where have you two travelled from and where are you going to?' Dorcon asked.

'We are travelling to the city to find and rescue my father. Our family name is Trueheart,' Tom said, 'we are adventurers.'

'Sit then, Tom Trueheart, bold young adventurer, and share some of this breakfast with me.'

There were olives and flat bread and a round of white goat's cheese on a vine leaf. Jollity sat watching over Tom and the road from his high branch.

'So you travel to the city to seek your father?' Dorcon asked.

'Yes,' said Tom. He was not absolutely sure he liked the bitter taste of the olives; he did like the goat's cheese though. 'My father is a brave man, a giant killer. I believe he is the prisoner of the king.'

'A giant killer, eh, now that's quite a boast. There are stories here of a giant, a giant made of golden brass. His name is Talos and he guards treasure on an island not too far away.'

'Really,' Tom said, 'a brass giant. How tall is he?'

'Taller than a mountain, they say. He walks around the island and the man who could defeat him would win treasure on earth and a place among the stars.'

'What is the name of this island?' Tom asked.

'It has no name, as far as I know, but it is a terrible place with a terrible secret, for a boy like you, of your age. Do not even think of going there.'

'Why?' said Tom.

The shepherd looked across at the distant hills and

the bright line of the sea, and played part of a sad little tune on his pipes, and then he said, 'Every so often six young men and six young women are taken there, and they never come back. Something terrible happens to them. Set to happen about this time of the year too; it will soon be time for the choosing. The king must choose, then off they all go on a ship with black sails.'

'The king chooses?'

'Oh yes. It is his duty, and a heavy burden, so heavy that the last king fled the kingdom nine years ago rather than do it.'

'I ought to go now,' Tom said, and he stood and brushed down his tunic. 'Thank you for sharing your food.'

'Before you go,' said Dorcon, 'I was hoping that you might help me with something.'

'If I can,' said Tom.

Dorcon reached into the bag at his waist and pulled out a little wax tablet covered with a leaf and tied with a posy of wild flowers.

'I am a shepherd, as you see, and I care for my flock. I play my flute here under the olive tree and I would not leave them alone, but I have an errand, a delivery

154

to make. I have written a poem while sitting here in the shade. I wonder if you could leave it in a certain place for me.'

'I will do my best,' said Tom. 'Where should I leave it?'

'The place is not far from the road you must travel. You see, I have lost my heart to a nymph; just leave this in a certain grove of trees for her to find and read.'

'That sounds just like my brothers, they lost their hearts to a lot of princesses. Is a nymph like a princess?' Tom asked.

'Very like,' said Dorcon, smiling. 'A few leagues from here you will pass a place where there is a perfect circle of dark trees. You should just be able to hear running water. Leave the poem on the flat stone in the middle of the trees. While you are there fill your water bottle; the water there is very good, very sweet.'

'I will,' said Tom, as he took the little parcel.

Jollity flew down and settled on Tom's shoulder.

'Are we off, Tom?' he said.

'Yes,' Tom said. 'I think we should get to the city now as soon as we can.'

'Take care, young man, and don't be in too much of

a hurry to play the hero,' said Dorcon, 'the roads to the city can be dangerous. There may be charlatans, monsters, pirates, brigands, robbers and all sorts. Keep your hand near your sword. I hope you find your father. Go with the gods.'

'I will,' said Tom, and he set off back down the slope while Jollity flew ahead scanning the roadway.

Tom tried to run some of the way but it was just too hot, and so he settled into as fast a walk as he could manage. He walked for a while on a shaded track in the grass under trees and bordered by wild flowers.

It was not long before Tom met some other travellers on the road coming in the other direction.

'Good morning,' Tom said in his cheery voice.

'Not so good around here,' said a man in a wine-coloured tunic. 'Monster on the loose.'

'Yes, watch out, young shaver,' said the other traveller, a kindly looking woman who carried a bundle of washing on her back.

'Monster?' Tom said.

'That's right, young feller-me-lad, a monster,' the man said. 'A cursed and fearsome beast, been seen near the town and we are not waiting around to find out more.'

'Needs a real hero to fight it,' the woman added. 'Maybe you know someone: an adventurer, a warrior, a soldier?'

'I am an adventurer myself,' Tom said. 'I am a Trueheart of the Adventuring Truehearts.'

'This beast needs a *real* adventurer to deal with it. No offence,' said the man, looking Tom up and down with a quizzical eye, 'but you'd best turn back now before it's too late.'

'Truehearts don't turn back,' said Tom bravely, but nervously.

Jollity landed on his shoulder and said, 'I admire your confidence, Tom, but shouldn't we see this creature before you decide to fight it?'

'Another monster,' said the man, pointing at Jollity the crow, 'a soothsaying bird, an ill omen.'

'Come on, this is no place for us,' said the woman. 'Pity, because you look like a nice useful lad. I could have done with someone like you to help me squeeze all the water out of my washing.'

'I'm an adventurer,' said Tom, 'not a washing squeezer helper boy.'

The man and the woman trudged away and the woman turned and waved to Tom. 'Good luck,' she said, 'you'll need it.' And then they were out of sight.

'You fly on ahead and tell me if you see anything of this monster,' said Tom.

Jollity flew up and away and Tom carried on along the pathway alone.

It was then that Tom saw the perfect circle of dark trees that Dorcon had mentioned. He stepped off the road and sure enough he could hear the trickle of water from somewhere in among the trees. And there was a flat rock in the very middle of the circle.

This must be the place, he thought. He took the little wax tablet out of his travel bag and laid it carefully on the stone. Then he went over to where the sound of the water was coming from. There was a faint waterfall spilling from some rocks hidden among the leaves. The water formed a dark pool and Tom knelt among the mossy rocks and gratefully drank some of the water. It was as delicious as Dorcon had promised. Then he filled one of his stone ginger beer bottles from the pond, stoppered it, and tucked it back into his packstaff bundle.

An old ragged man, with a long white beard, stepped out from the deep shadow of the trees. 'You have drunk from these waters,' he said, his arms raised. 'Be blessed, young traveller,' he added.

'Thank you, sir,' said Tom. 'I needed that, it's hot work walking these roads. I feel much better now.'

'That water will do more than quench a traveller's thirst. It will do more than make you feel better,' the man said. 'Beware the labyrinth and the bull,' he added mysteriously.

'Sorry, sir, but what do you mean?' Tom asked. 'Who are you?'

'I am an oracle, I foresee all; I tell the future. I have seen the golden giant, the dark king, the ship with black sails.' He bowed and backed away again among the thick leaves.

'How much more will the water do?' Tom called out. 'You speak in riddles.' He was puzzled and vaguely worried, but there was no reply; the old man seemed to have gone.

He had looked a little like the forest hermit back in the Land of Stories, the forest hermit who had taught Tom his letters and numbers; so perhaps they had hermits here too?

He tucked his packstaff back over his shoulder and walked on towards the town. As he walked he tried testing his abilities to see if he could find any difference after drinking the water from the spring. He stopped on the path and jumped into the air; he looked into the shadows under the trees, but he could jump no higher, and see no more clearly than usual. In fact, disappointingly, he felt just the same as ever and so he dismissed what the old man had said as nonsense.

He knew he was getting nearer to the town by the sounds. Cries of panic and thunderous roaring noises drifted through the warm air. A woman's voice called out 'Help!' Jollity flew down and settled suddenly on Tom's shoulder in a flurry of wings.

'Oh, you made me jump just then, Jollity, suddenly landing on me like that,' Tom said.

'Sorry, Tom, but you'll jump even more when you

see what I just saw; it's a really horrible thing,' said Jollity. At that moment a great clap of thunder came from the sky.

They crested a hill and a fine looking town was laid out below them. White villas and green gardens, all hot and sleepy looking in the patches of sunlight. There were great grey clouds too boiling up overhead.

Tom could see a nervous crowd of people ranged along the streets around the very edges of the town square. Somewhere in the centre he could see a creature. It looked like a hunched-over man, an especially large one, and it was working with a huge hammer at an enormous anvil.

'See what I mean, Tom?' said Jollity.

'Yes I do,' said Tom. 'What is it doing?'

'Watch,' Jollity said.

The creature roared something out and then straightened and took something bright from the top of the anvil and flung its arm outwards and upwards. A huge bolt of lightning shot up into the sky from his arm. It shot above the town and crashed up into the rolling grey clouds. The crowds in the streets shrank back further as the creature's head turned to face them. There were screams and there was a great crash of thunder in the sky, and a bolt of lightning shot back down out of the clouds. It was a jagged streak of yellow-white light and as the light passed by the creature Tom saw it clearly for the first time. It had just one eye right in the middle of its forehead.

'What on earth is that?' said Tom.

'That is a Cyclops, Tom, a one-eyed giant.'

The Cyclops roared again and hammered away at his anvil; picked up another lightning bolt and sent it up into the clouds. Another shattering crash of thunder followed and another bolt of lightning travelled out of the sky and this one struck one of the buildings with a crash and a burst of flames.

'We must try and stop him,' Tom said. 'Come on.'

Tom made his way down the hill quickly with Jollity riding on his shoulder. He started making his way through the streets where little groups of frightened looking townspeople were hiding as best they could.

'Careful, young man, you stay here with us,' said a kindly looking lady. 'It's dangerous out there.'

'Where is the hero to save us from this?' said the man next to her. 'They are never around when you need one. They are happy enough to pose for their statues and pictures on vases and the like, but when something like this happens . . . ' The man shook his head.

The thunder blasted out again, followed by a flash of bright light and screams.

'I am an adventurer,' said Tom, 'of the Adventuring Truehearts; perhaps I could help.'

'Have you been sent by the gods, or the terrible new king?' the man asked.

'He's only a boy,' said the kindly lady, 'you can see that.'

'This boy has carried out some very brave exploits,'

said Jollity staring at the frightened pair with his dark
eyes. They both staggered back in shock.

'A talking bird,' the man said. 'More sorcery, more
evil. This young boy is bewitched too.' And he turned
his head away. 'Don't look at them,' he added.

Jollity flew up and over the rooftops. Tom walked
on into the centre of the town. A tall broad man
followed him. He walked carefully, some way behind
Tom, and the man's head was all hooded over and shadowed. He edged his way carefully behind him as Tom
threaded his way through the frightened crowd.

The hooded figure pushed Tom from behind and
shoved him forward, and Tom emerged from the
crowd, from the tangle of arms and legs, and out into
open space. The crowd drew back even further behind
him like a tide, leaving Tom looking very small and
exposed as if on an empty beach, with his shadow
spilling across the white stone of the roadway as another
flash of lightning lit everything up.

The Cyclops turned its huge head, noticed Tom
standing all on his own and let out a low rumbling
growl. The single eye stared down at him, transfixed
him. Tom stood rooted to the spot. He felt the great

heat of the flames and the afternoon sun; he felt sweat trickle down between his narrow shoulderblades. Here was a mythical monster and it was somehow much worse looking than even the Norse dragon had been. At least Tom had seen pictures of all kinds of dragons before. He had never seen anything like this.

The monster stepped forward, its angry eye clearly fixed on Tom. The crowd were silent now all around and behind him except for the sound of their sandalled feet shuffling backwards on the stone. The Cyclops took another loping step forward. Jollity flew down from one of the buildings. He flew round the beast's head, and the Cyclops lashed out at the crow. Jollity flew up just in time and escaped.

'Careful, Tom,' he called out before he flew back up among the roofs.

This caused a murmur to pass through the frightened crowd. Tom heard the whispered word 'sorcerer'.

He kept his eyes fixed on the Cyclops; he could feel his legs shaking. He felt small, lost, and alone.

He looked down at his own stretched-out shadow. It loomed and quivered across the stone and it seemed to point straight at the Cyclops like an accusing finger.

There were some terracotta jars upturned on the ground and some spilled oil mingled with a puddle of water making a swirling rainbow pattern. Tom snapped to, he had to do something. He put his pack-staff slowly down on the ground, all the time watching the awful giant beast. Then Tom straightened very slowly and reached his hand down to his sword. He pulled it from the scabbard, again very slowly. It sparked and flared a little in the low sunlight. There was another murmur from the crowd at the sight of the white light rippling across the blade and this time he heard the word 'Hero' being muttered.

'Hero,' he said to himself. 'It's up to me now to be just that, to be as brave as my brothers.'

He took a step towards the monstrous Cyclops. He held his sword out straight in front of him with both hands. He hoped that the creature would perhaps leap forward and impale itself on the blade. The crowd fell silent again. There was a sense of watchful tension in the air as the young would-be hero and the one-eyed monster faced one another. The crowd were almost beginning to enjoy themselves. Jollity flew off from the roof and hovered over the Cyclops. With a cracking sound like a whiplash the Cyclops threw a thunderbolt from its hand. It missed Jollity but landed with a loud quivering crash on a wooden roof. Flames shot up briefly and the crowd screamed.

The Cyclops turned away from Tom and picked up the huge hammer from the anvil. It crashed away at something while Tom stood ready with his raised sword, unsure of what to expect or what he should do. The Cyclops turned and Tom saw that it was holding a sword made of what looked like beaten lightning. It lifted the sword with both hands and advanced towards Tom, who backed instinctively as a lightning flash whistled past him from the sword into the crowd, followed by screams of panic.

Another bolt flew past him just above his head and smashed into the wall of a house with a deafening crack. The Cyclops's aim was not good, but the lightning was lethal looking and wherever it hit flames shot upwards. Tom held his sword up in the air in front of him like a fence post and it deflected yet another series of bolts or sparks.

The Cyclops lifted its head high, shook it from side to side, and roared out something and Tom could clearly see its rotten looking teeth. So close was it that Tom could even smell the creature now, and it smelled like fire, hot metal, and sparks. Jollity circled round just above the monster's head, safely out of range but close enough to annoy it.

'It can't track me very well, Tom, with just the one eye,' said Jollity and flew up and off out of reach.

The Cyclops reared up with the lightning sword in both hands. It leapt upwards but couldn't quite reach Jollity who veered away higher. The Cyclops's mouth snarled and snappped up at Jollity. The Cyclops roared in fury and turned back to its huge anvil.

Tom, almost without thinking, ran forward with his eyes closed, his heart full of dread, and rammed his sparking sword hard up against something.

It was the anvil.

There was an immediate effect. There was the sound of an explosion. The crowd screamed and stepped back still further as what seemed like another huge clap of thunder rang out, and the Cyclops's anvil split in two. Tom opened his eyes: on the ground in front of him were the two halves of the iron anvil.

A great cheer went up from the crowd of townspeople. The Cyclops turned and faced Tom. He stepped over the broken anvil and moved forward with the lightning sword raised. The Cyclops slashed out with it and it crackled with energy as bright sparks shot past Tom. The sparks showered on to the ground and a flame shot up from the spilled oil. The line of fire moved quickly towards the crowd, who screamed again and stepped back still further, and there were cries of 'Fire!'

Tom raised his sword and the Cyclops parried it away at once with a single blow of the lightning sword so that Tom's sword skittered across the ground. The Cyclops roared something, and Tom ran backwards, to where his sword lay. The Cyclops turned its back again on Tom. It picked up one half of its broken anvil and threw it up into the air over the heads of the crowd and they scattered as it crashed to the ground.

The fire made an almost complete circle around Tom. He reached down and picked up his bow and his quiver of arrows. He fixed an arrow to the string of his bow and pulled back hard. He fired the arrow at the Cyclops and it struck home. The Cyclops turned then as if it had been stung. Tom fired another arrow quickly and the Cyclops parried it away with the crackle of his lightning sword. It was not enough. Tom stepped backwards again while the Cyclops threw more thunderbolts and lightning flashes out at the crowd. Tom noticed that the Cyclops avoided the fire, was perhaps even confused by it. Jollity's right, Tom thought, it can't judge distances with one eye, to the monster it is all flat.

Tom pulled the square of Trueheart cloth that his father had left for him out of his travel bag. He tore it in two very quickly, and fixed one half around the shaft of an arrow near the tip. He held it to the flames and the fabric caught. He raised the bow and aimed at the Cyclops. He loosed the arrow. The arc of flame sped towards the Cyclops. It struck home somewhere near its eye and then fell and caught on the creature's rough leather tunic. The Cyclops screamed, put a hand over his eye, and fell back on to the ground.

Another giant man suddenly loomed out of the edge of the crowd, a huge man with a hood over his head. Tom could see enough of the man's face to recognize at once that it was surely the stitched-faced man, Ormestone's hideous henchman. The man doused the flames on the Cyclops's tunic. Tom fired another arrow and the stiched-faced man batted it away. Tom fired another. The crowd cheered. The Cyclops dropped the lightning sword, and it seemed to dissolve away on the stone. Tom's shadow was suddenly sharp and clear, pointing once again like an accusing finger at the Cyclops huddled on the ground.

The stitched-faced man helped the great wounded creature back up on to its feet. They stood for a moment together; both were of a similar build and height. The Cyclops reached down for its sword but the sword had now completely dissolved away, leaving a tang of burnt sulphur smell in the air, just like the Norse dragon.

The oil fire around Tom died down too, and the crowd, sensing the unexpected defeat of the Cyclops, roared and cheered, and the word 'Hero' rose out of the crowd more than once. Someone threw a vegetable at the Cyclops, and more followed from the crowd. The stitched-faced man draped his own cloak over the hunched monster revealing his own terrible face. A gasp went up from the crowd at the sight of him. The bowed Cyclops howled something out into the sky as another vegetable hit him on the head, and then another. The stiched-faced man moved slowly away taking the Cyclops with him. The crowd roared and booed as the two of them walked out of the town square and up one of the empty side streets.

The crowd surged forward around Tom.

Tom felt himself lifted up and carried on someone's shoulder. 'He's a hero all right,' shouted one voice.

'Sent from Zeus himself,' called out another.

Tom struggled back down to the ground. 'Where's my friend?' he called out.

The crow flew down and settled on Tom's shoulder.

'Jollity,' Tom said, 'you saw who rescued the Cyclops?'

'Indeed I did, Tom, and well done with the bow and arrows.'

'See how he talks to that bird,' came a voice from the excited crowd.

'That bird talks back to him. I saw them talking together earlier,' said another voice. 'That boy is indeed sent from the gods.'

For the moment, Tom ignored the excitement and everything and everyone around him. He stroked Jollity on the neck very lightly with the tip of his finger. 'Come on, old friend,' he said. 'Time to move on.'

Chapter 16

King Ormestone surveyed the throne room at his palace with one of his wide and sinister smiles. He had quickly surrounded himself with as much of the royal gold as he could find in the dark recesses of the palace strongroom coffers. The whole of his throne room glittered now with gold and golden reflections. There were gold plate, gold goblets, golden mirrors, and heaped up in a chest on the centre table was the dragon's stolen hoard.

Ormestone smiled, not only at the beauty of his gold, but also at the fact that he had had Big Jack Trueheart moved from his villa by soldiers and he was even now safely locked away in the lowest dungeon chambers. He smiled too at the cunning plan he had just hatched with Rumpelstiltskin of how to finally be rid of the rest of the meddling Truehearts. He busily wrapped himself in his best royal cloak which was then smoothed over by faithful Rumpelstiltskin.

'You promise me, master, that I shall see my princesses again,' he said.

'See them you shall,' said Ormestone slyly. 'Why, I shall send you along to help fetch them. Those brothers will need quelling after all, all of them.'

Ormestone told Rumpelstiltskin to wait. 'I am going to visit our prisoner before we leave.'

'Hurry back, sire, your majesty,' came the voice of Rumpelstiltskin.

Ormestone found Big Jack Trueheart sitting in the dungeon room deep below in the rock heart of the palace. A sprite lion was lying across the floor in front of the barred doorway. It lifted its head when Ormestone came in and it made a growling sound and stretched and yawned and showed its teeth. Jack was manacled to the rock wall. Ormestone watched him for a while through the bars of the dungeon cell.

'My patience with you and your kind is thin, it will only last for so long,' he said, icily. He raised his finger and thumb and held them very close together as if to show just how thin.

Jack said nothing but stared gloomily at the floor of the cell.

'I am leaving for an appointment,' Ormestone continued, 'which I am confident will finally lead to the downfall of your brutish sons and their silly princess wives.'

'Oh,' said Jack, looking up at Ormestone with a level gaze, his eyes sharply blue behind his spectacles, 'so they are all finally married at last then. That is good and happy news indeed.'

'Is that all you have to say?' Ormestone replied, thrown by Jack's fierce level gaze.

'I just wondered how you knew,' said Jack quietly.

'I have my methods,' said Ormestone. 'I am afraid that you too will be sacrificed along with them.'

'Sacrificed?' said Jack, his voice rising.

'We are, after all, in the Land of Myths and Legends,' said Ormestone. 'A place of ice and a place of heat and a place of blood and earth, a place of ancient beliefs

176

and stories. Oh, and such wonderfully unhappy stories too. There will, and must, be sacrifices of blood. I know of one that is just perfect for my needs, and what an ending it will have.'

'There will, of course, be heroes here too,' said Jack.

'I wouldn't count on that,' said Ormestone. 'Who were you imagining, your little boy Tom perhaps?' And he laughed his chilling laugh and the guard lion roared once in echo. Big Jack blocked his ears and so did not hear the door being shut with a final clang.

After Ormestone had gone Jack sat up straight and took a few twists of paper from his pocket and a little cloth bag which he put into a gap in the stone wall.

After Ormestone had locked the door shut a voice echoed from the rock walls about him.

'Hurry, sire.'

'How dare you speak to me in that way,' Ormestone shouted angrily up the stairs.

'I am sorry, sire, your majesty, your highness,' said Rumpelstiltskin, 'it is just that sails have been reported on the horizon. Those pirates we sent so wonderfully off course are now close.'

'It was a very clever idea of yours to send that Story Bureau letter to one of the captains at The Olde Admiral Benbow Inne. Amazing what a small piece of sprite gold can do as a bribe placed in the right villainous hands, or should I rather say hook? Interfering with the charts to bring them here, straight to us too. They will soon be doing exactly as I ask. Are the soldiers all in place?'

'I believe so, your majesty, and I will see my princesses soon, won't I,' and he looked up at Ormestone like a puppy.

'Come then, to the harbour, and stop looking at me like that, you look disgusting,' Ormestone replied, sweeping past the little sprite, who trotted down the shining marble corridor after his master.

'I was just wondering, sire,' said Rumpelstiltskin, desperately trying to change the subject, 'sorry, your majesty, how your Cyclops beast was faring out in the world?'

'A useful trap that, a trap to catch a brave little hero,' and Ormestone laughed his cruel laugh.

'And also, your majesty, surely a good way of dealing with troublemakers too.'

'Oh indeed it is,' said Ormestone.

They set off out of the palace into the harsh sunlight, and Rumpelstiltskin muttered under his breath, 'Oh, the terrible heat of this place,' and then said how he longed for a 'nice fresh cold northern pine forest'.

Adelphos, the captain of the guard, saluted them both and then fell in step beside them as they made their way down the palace steps into the narrow sunlit streets to the harbour. The streets had been emptied of people. An occasional shutter creaked open at a window, or the broad leaves of a plant on a balcony were pulled aside as the king and his entourage passed through the town. People watched and waited from the quiet safety of their homes. There was a hushed expectant atmosphere. Something serious was up.

At the harbour a great crowd of heavily armed warriors

stood hidden among the shadows of the buildings and wharves.

'They are all set, sire, as you see,' Adelphos said as he bowed before Ormestone. 'You can see the sails. There is just the one ship but of an unusual shape and type.'

He pointed out to sea and Ormestone saw a three-masted sailing ship with a skull and crossbones flag.

'Someone seems to have wandered wildly off course,' he said to Rumpelstiltskin with a grin. 'What a shock they will get. Almost worth the bribes I had to pay out to that villain to see their faces when they realize they are not where they think they are, and that this is not the kind of harbour they were expecting.'

'No, master, so much the better,' Rumpelstiltskin said.

There came a bright flash of fire from the side of the ship, followed by an explosion like thunder and then a tearing sound as if the air itself was being ripped open by a giant claw, and then a great cloud of smoke erupted from the side of the ship.

'Down,' Ormestone shouted, but the captain of the

guard just stood amazed as a heavy cannonball tore overhead and smashed into one of the wooden roofs, splintering it and sending fragments of dust and timber spinning up in the air.

'What weapon is that?' he said in a shocked and awestruck voice. 'By Zeus it is surely fire from the gods themselves.' And he fell to his knees and added breathlessly, 'These are not our usual pirates.'

'Never mind that, hide yourself, man,' Ormestone shouted.

There were no more warning shots from the ship's cannon. The ship docked and a fierce looking crowd of scurvy cut-throats and vagabonds came ashore. They looked around at the buildings with puzzled faces. Their leader, a ragged man in a tricorn hat, with an eyepatch and a wooden peg-leg and a brightly coloured parrot on his shoulder, called out, 'Steady now, lads, this yere is a strange place but looks like there'll be rich pickings for all.'

The crew advanced across the smooth stone of the harbour arm, their weapons, flintlock pistols, cutlasses, daggers, and muskets held out threateningly in front of them.

'No one here at all,' said one pirate who wore a gold earring in each ear.

'It's a ghost town,' said another. The pirates stopped as a group and looked at the fine marble buildings that climbed the hill towards the royal palace, all dazzling white and magnificent in the sunlight.

There came the sound of a drum being struck, a great bass thump which echoed loudly around the stone buildings. This was answered by the shrill cry of a brass hunting horn, a wild and ancient-sounding fanfare, a few crude notes and then the thunder of the drum came again. And then it seemed as if all the shadows moved out from under the buildings and a sudden and enormous armoured army began to surround the pirates. They stretched all around the harbour area in a closing circle, men in shining helms and breastplates, carrying swords or spears.

'Well, lads,' said the man with the peg-leg showing a mouthful of gold teeth, ' 'ere's a mystery, we seem to have travelled off course or something. There's an awful lot of 'em but do your best . . . arrggh.'

He raised his cutlass in the air and one of his crew fired a musket at the line of armoured soldiers. The response was a hail of arrows which seemed to come from nowhere out of the bright enamel-blue sky. The pirates threw themselves down on the ground and huddled close together in terror as the phalanx of armoured men marched in time to the trumpet and drum and steadily surrounded them.

'Weapons away, I think, lads,' the peg-legged pirate said. 'There's just too durned many of 'em.'

Within a few short seconds each of the grumbling and fearful ragged pirates found himself staring up close at the sharp point of either a sword or spear and into the fiercely armoured faces of warriors from the ancient world.

Ormestone strode across the open square beyond the harbour and the warriors bowed as one, like a wave breaking, as he passed. He confronted the group of cowering pirates. 'Stand up,' he said, and the crew shuffled up and stood nervously looking around. 'I am the king here,' Ormestone said. He waited, there was little response from the dirty unshaven faces of the pirate crew. 'You may well cower; you are common pirates and you have come here to pillage the coffers of my palace, and don't deny it.'

'Don't even know what this place is, 't ain't where we was headed, it ain't Port-o'-Spain and that's a fact,' said the pirate captain.

'Pirates were expected and pirates you are, and your intention is always to steal treasure.'

'Not always,' the peg-legged pirate replied. 'Sometimes we just find buried things and return them to the rightful owners, and anyway, who are you callin' common?'

'You, of course,' said Ormestone. 'Buried treasure, you mean?'

'Aye,' the captain added doubtfully. 'Doubloons and suchlike.'

The bright bird perched on his shoulder called out, 'Pieces of eight, pieces of eight.'

'I can offer you all just the one simple choice,' Ormestone said.

'A choice, eh, 'tween what and what?'

'A choice between death on the one hand' . . . Ormestone paused, gesturing to the surrounding soldiers, 'or gold doubloons on the other,' he continued.

With a clatter of metal the circle of warriors extended their sharp blades just a little closer to the pirates' throats.

The peg-legged pirate turned to his companions. 'Hear that, lads, aarrrgh, he offers us a choice, 'tis 'tween doubloons and death.'

'Ain't no choice at all,' said one.

'Pieces of eight,' cried the bright bird.

'Thank 'ee, your majesty, on calm reflection we'll take your doubloons, though I doubt there's any honour in it. You may not know it but we do have our own code of honour.'

'No doubt,' said Ormestone. 'Very wise, very wise indeed. Now, you will come under escort to the palace and you will listen very carefully to what I have to say.'

Chapter 17

The sun was low in the sky and the sea was warm and calm. Rapunzel, Cinderella, Princess Zinnia, Sleeping Beauty and Snow White and Jack's wife Jill (who had once been under a wicked enchantment as a common or garden carthorse) were walking along the shoreline, at Club Happy Ever After. They were paddling in the gentle surf as it rolled and foamed up on to the soft white sand of the beach. Each carried her pretty wedding shoes in one hand, and a fine lacy parasol to protect her skin from the sun in the other. It was a warm evening and further up the beach their adoring, adventuring, Trueheart husbands were sitting in a proud line watching them. Jack waved down to Jill and Jill waved her pretty little wedding shoes back at Jack.

'Must make a change from horseshoes, I bet,' said Princess Zinnia with a sly grin, nodding at Jill's shoes.

'It really does,' said Jill, who could not quite escape the fact that she wasn't a princess like some of the others.

'Clippity-clop,' said Snow White, 'clippity-clop.'

'Now, girls, don't let's be mean to Jill,' said Rapunzel, squinting out at the bright sea where the dark shape of a fast sailing ship could now be seen. 'Look at that,' she said.

'If I didn't know any better,' said Cinderella, 'I would say that was a pirate ship.'

'Not here, surely,' said Sleeping Beauty. 'Not near the island of Happy Ever After.'

The girls all stopped paddling and looked out to sea from under the edge of their parasols. The boat was sailing fast towards the shore and there was no doubt as to what it was. They could clearly see the large black flag with the stark white skull and crossbones flying from the mainmast. The ship seemed to be close to bearing down on their paradise beach.

Jack Trueheart was the first of the adventurers to notice the ship. He stood and pointed across the water. 'That don't seem right, that big old pirate ship like that heading for our beach.'

'No, it doesn't,' said Jacquot, 'and look at us unarmed and all.'

'It's heading into shore, straight for us,' said Jackson.

'I don't like this at all,' said Jackie.

'Nor do I,' said Jake. 'This isn't meant to happen here, it's against all the rules.'

'As fast as we can then,' said Jacques.

They leapt up in unison and ran down the sloping beach kicking up great clouds of white sand. As soon as they were with their wives, Jackie said, 'Shouldn't one of us go back to the palace for our weapons?'

'Too late,' said Rapunzel with a sigh, 'look.'

With lightning speed, the pirate ship had already anchored in the shallow water off the beach. A group of scruffy pirates stood in the prow pointing muskets and pistols directly at the Truehearts and their brides, while a crowd of even more fiercely armed pirates were splashing towards them through the curling foam.

The Truehearts had a choice: raise their arms in surrender, or fight.

Princess Zinnia snapped shut her parasol and then suddenly ran forward fearlessly through the water with a whoop. She held the furled lace parasol out in front of her like a sword. The other brides followed at once, each one using her parasol as a weapon.

The brothers Trueheart waded in. There was confusion in the water. Brides piled on pirates, whacking out with their parasols. They cuffed bandanaed heads, they pulled at gold earrings, they fended off and parried cutlass blows. The pirates were dumbfounded. They hadn't expected anyone to fight back, especially the princesses. The burly brothers were fit and rested, and they soon sent some pirates down hard into the water with their beefy fists.

'Take that, you scurvy knave,' Jack shouted as he walloped a pirate who had several big gold earrings in each ear.

There were shouts from the ship: 'Remember now, lads, keep 'em alive, 'e wants 'em alive and kicking.'

Jack tore himself free from the pirate that had hold of him, and looked up at the ship. The pirate who had just shouted had a bright parrot on his shoulder and a crutch under one arm. The brothers and their brides fought bravely for a little longer; the girls were lashing out with their parasols still, as best they could, but without weapons they were soon overpowered. Eventually the pirates had them quelled and lined up along the shoreline. The pirates certainly hadn't had it all their own way, one or two were nursing bruised heads, and worse: bruised pride. Beaten by young women in sun dresses with only parasols for weapons.

Moments later the pirate captain limped through the surf on his peg-leg and crutch. 'Pieces of eight,' the parrot called out from his shoulder. It was then that

Jack noticed a little figure walking behind the pirate, with a circlet of leaves on his straggle-haired head, and a gnarled little stick held out in his hand.

'Oh no,' said Jack. 'I ought to have known it.'

'Known what?' said Jill, still struggling in the grip of a fierce looking pirate.

'That it would be something to do with *him*,' Jack said, nodding his head in the direction of the little sprite.

The girls all gasped as one. 'Rumply,' Zinnia called out, 'is that you?'

'Ne'er you mind Rumply,' said the pirate captain. 'We're sent here under threat and against our pirate's honour to take you to visit an old friend of yours.'

'Ormestone,' said Jackie.

'Arrgghh, that's the one, the king hisself,' said the pirate. 'If we don't take yer then half my crew of good lads what we left behind 'll be strung up and hanged from the yardarm.' He gestured to Rumpelstiltskin. 'If you wouldn't mind.'

Rumpelstiltskin had been momentarily overcome with a surge of joy at seeing his beloved girls all lined up in their pretty summer dresses. He raised his stick, which trembled in his hand, and hesitated.

It was just enough time for Jack to break free from the small pirate that held him and stumble forward into the surf with a murderous look in his eyes. He stretched his arms out towards Rumpelstiltskin but before he could reach him, in an instant, iron manacles and chains snapped suddenly and brutally around his wrists and ankles and he fell forward into the surf. His brothers and their brides were all chained together in the exact same way, a split second later.

'Not again,' Rapunzel called out to Rumpelstiltskin, holding up her chained wrists, but the sprite made no reply. He just smiled and tucked his head shyly into the collar of his cloak. The pirates pushed and pulled the Truehearts back through the surf and bundled them up to the pirate ship where they all awkwardly climbed the rope ladder up on to the deck.

There they stood in a wet and ragged line. Jacquot shouted, 'This is the sacred Island of Happy Ever After, you can't invade this place, let us all go at once.'

'That king 'e don't play by your rules, or ours even,' said the pirate captain. 'I regrets it meself, 'tis dirty work e'en though we is pirates. Ain't no honour in it, aaaargh.'

The parrot on his shoulder said, 'Pieces of eight, pieces of eight.'

'But there is gold, yer see, and my own lads' survival. To be sure, the king has kept hold of some of us as insurance. He 'as us all over a barrel. Take 'em below,' the captain said. 'We're off back to where we came from.'

'And where is that?' asked Cinderella.

'The Land of Myths and Legends,' said Rumpel-stiltskin quietly. 'Far away from here, my poor lovely.'

Chapter 18

Tom shouldered his packstaff and turned away from the crowd. It was time to go and find his father. The crowd of excited and grateful towns-people parted around him to let him through. A woman stepped in front of him and blocked his path.

'You saved us, young man,' she said, 'from that awful thing. You bested him, you broke him, you are a hero, a real hero.' There were agreements from among the crowd.

'You saved us from the Cyclops,' said another excited voice.

'Yes, the Cyclops,' another repeated. There were loud cheers.

'That beast you defeated was horrible and would have destroyed our little town, were it not for you,' said another.

'Hero,' a man's voice called out from behind him, and another. 'Hero,' they all cried out. Tom tried to walk away through the crowd.

'Wait,' someone called to him.

Tom walked on, and as he walked people patted him on the shoulder, and he kept hearing that word 'hero', again and again. He had reached the very edge of the crowd when another man's voice called out.

'Stay and be our own hero, young man?'

'No, I am sorry,' said Tom. 'You see I am not a hero I am just a simple boy adventurer doing his best to find his lost father.'

The crowd let out a deafening cheer, and Tom and Jollity found themselves hoisted up on to someone's shoulders while Jollity held on tight to Tom. They were paraded around the street for a while as the crowd cheered them again and again.

Jollity finally took off from Tom's shoulder and

briefly circled over the crowd in the sunlight. There was no sign of the terrible stitched-faced man or the fearful Cyclops.

'You are a true hero as well as an adventurer,' one well-wisher said.

Jollity flew back and said, 'Come on now, Tom, time we set off.'

A member of the crowd stepped forward and said, 'I can offer you shelter at my villa; join us for a cele-bration, for a feast, young hero.'

'I am afraid we cannot, we have urgent business in the city,' Tom said. 'How far away is the city?'

'At least two days' and nights' walking,' said the man, 'and I should warn you that the road to the city is a dangerous one.'

'We are already well warned, sir,' said Tom, 'thank you.'

Tom hoisted his packstaff.

'Thank you again, young man, for saving us,' the man said. 'Where may we say you were from?'

'I am Tom Trueheart of the Adventuring Truehearts. 'We are from the Land of Stories.'

'The Land of Stories,' said the man, puzzled. 'I

confess I have never heard of such a place. Is it beyond Ephesus, north of Phrygia perhaps, or south of Sparta?'

'I have never heard of those places,' said Tom.

'It seems we come from two different worlds,' the man said. 'Now I look at you even your clothes seem odd, rougher even than a local shepherd or a goat herder, and yet you are well armed with a fine sword?'

'Tom,' said Jollity, 'too many questions.' And as he said it he held his head on one side and nodded.

Tom realized that Jollity meant him to be a little more suspicious. That they could not simply trust everyone who was nice to them, or who asked them questions.

'We really must go now,' Tom said, and he turned away from the crowd. He waved his hand in goodbye and another great roar went up. Jollity flew up in the air and on ahead while Tom turned and set off, following the road out of the town with his packstaff tucked jauntily over his shoulder.

Chapter 19

Tom and Jollity travelled until the evening, and here the darkness came on swiftly. There was almost no twilight as there would have been at home. The night sky was clear and full of stars. Tom had never paid that much attention to the stars and the constellations at home. The skies above the Land of Stories were frequently hidden by mists and frets and thick clouds, so that the night skies were often murky, and the stars invisible. Now, walking through the warm night, he kept looking up and marvelling at the stars, so many of them, thousands of bright pinpricks of light shining above them in the deep black sky.

'All those stars,' he said to Jollity. 'So many of them and so clear. I have never seen a night sky like that.'

'Yes, Tom,' said Jollity, 'it's amazing. Look, the starlight is bright enough to see the road by.'

'And they make shapes that look like things,' Tom said.

'Do they?' said Jollity.

'Yes, look up there where I am pointing. If you follow my finger, that lot there look like a bear; you can see the shape.'

'Can't see it myself.'

'Yes you can, look again. The bear's head is looking down at us and that straight line of stars is his back and you can see his legs, there and there.' He pointed again at the sky.

'Cicero says they named some of the groups of stars after heroes in ancient stories,' Jollity said, his beak pointing up at the sky. 'No, I still can't make out a bear; maybe a horse.'

'Ancient stories?' said Tom.

'Myths and stories from this very place, I suppose he meant,' said Jollity.

'That dragon, or the giant wolf Fenrir, may be up

there somewhere then, or that terrible beast the Cyclops,' said Tom.

'I think he meant heroes and heroines, and gods and goddesses, that sort of thing,' said Jollity.

'Heroes like my dad, like Big Jack; they might name stars after him?' Tom said.

'They might,' said Jollity, 'or they might name some after you, Tom, if you manage to save your father and bring him back. That really would be quite a story.'

'Oh, I'll bring him back all right,' said Tom.

They settled by the side of the road. There was no need for shelter, the night was warm, and under the sky of stories Tom finally fell asleep trying his best to make figures and heroes out of the clusters of bright stars.

Chapter 20

TOWARDS THE CITY

8.13 A.M.

Tom and Jollity set off early before the sun was too hot.

Tom was almost completely lost in thought, and Jollity was flying high overhead, when a group of roughly dressed figures stepped out from among the trees and on to the road, barring the way.

Tom walked right into one of them before he noticed them at all.

'Not so fast,' came a thick low voice.

Tom staggered back and finally took in the line of ruffians spread out across the roadway all around him. They closed in, blocking his way both forward and back. Out of the corner of his eye Tom noticed Jollity glide silently down among the trees near the side of the road.

A silence fell, broken only by the scritching of the cicadas, and the hot wind rustling through the turning leaves.

Finally the man Tom had bumped up against said, 'Where are you going in such a hurry, my young boy?'

Tom took a step backwards. 'I am on my way to the city,' he said. 'Now please let me pass.'

'I am not sure we can let you pass, I think we may need to extract a toll from you. Now whatever you have in that travel bag, or wrapped up in that silly thing on the end of the stick, just hand it all over now.'

'I can't do that,' Tom said.

'Can't or won't?' said the man.

'Both,' said Tom defiantly, surprising himself.

The man pulled a sword from his belt, and at the same moment all the others crowded around Tom drew their swords too with a metallic swish.

'You're brigands,' said Tom.

'Clever little boy,' the man said and laughed a big

roar of a laugh, as did all the others. 'And what do brigands do, eh, lad?' he added.

'I don't know,' said Tom nervously, moving his hand as slowly as he could down towards the handle of his birthday sword. Dorcon the shepherd had been right about the road to the city.

'I'll tell you what brigands do, shall I, boy,' the man said. 'They meet rude little boys on the road, little boys just like you, and then they take those rude little boys off somewhere dark and they cut them up into pieces with rusted hatchets and blunt knives as slow as they like. And then they put the pieces in a pot and cook 'em up for breakfast, that's what brigands do.'

The brigand grinned from ear to ear, pleased at his blood-curdling description of the horrors that waited for boys like Tom. He bent his head close to Tom and noticed that Tom was wet with sweat pouring from his brow.

'Why, look at the little shrimp, men, 'e looks like he's cooking already. Hot enough for you, boy? Now give over the valuables.'

'I have no valuables,' said Tom.

'We'll be the judge of that, now turf it all out.'

Reluctantly Tom tipped the contents of his travel bag out on to the road. There wasn't much there: Hafnir's folded cloak with the wolf pelt, some scraps of food and some maps.

The brigand stepped close to the little pile. He poked at the thick cloak and then he hooked it up on the end of his sword and waved it. 'Look at this, a nice warm winter cloak, shame not to be wearing it on such a cold morning as this, eh, little feller.' He could see even more sweat running down Tom's face as he stood trembling in the scorching sunlight. The brigand roared with laughter, and so did all the other brigands. 'I think you had better put this on, lad, warm you up a bit. Well, go on then,' he said dropping the cloak at Tom's feet, 'we may as well keep you cooking now you've started.'

Looking reluctant Tom took up the heavy cloak and fastened the thick fur collar at his neck.

'I bet that feels better already, eh?' the brigand said chuckling at Tom's discomfort.

Tom was able to grasp the handle of his sword beneath the cover of the cloak.

'Ooh look, a bottle of something. Water, or something stronger, I wonder?' said the brigand leader, and he held the stone bottle up high in the bright sunlight. It was then that Jollity swooped down out of the sky and snatched the ginger beer bottle straight out of the brigand's meaty hand.

At the same moment Tom suddenly pulled his sword free from the stifling fur-edged cloak and it flashed and dazzled like a mirror in the bright air. The brigand staggered backwards, and roared, 'Get 'im.' He tried to land a blow with his own sword but it bounced off the cloak and then Tom parried it, and sliced through the brigand's sword blade as if it were a round of goat's cheese.

'What the . . . ' The brigand looked down in shock at the handle and stump left in his great hairy paw.

Despite the terrible heat inside the cloak, Tom's arm felt strong now, energized. Without stopping to see the effect of his first blow he moved fast, straight at the other brigands to the side of him. He sliced through the handle of an axe, and then a brigand brought his hatchet down in a swift movement and it too bounced harmlessly off the cloak from Tom's shoulder. Tom felt nothing. Other blows were quickly turned aside by the cloak too, and all the while Tom worked through the line of brigands, hacking and chopping at their weapons with his sword. His arm felt stronger with every blow. The brigands fought back in shock, but every blow, slice, or hack they struck at Tom did nothing. The cloak protected him; they might as well have just been tickling him with feathers. Tom whirled and turned. He moved furiously forwards up the road getting in among and beyond the gang of brigands. In a second he was out on the other side of the line, looking back at them. They were all spread out in shock and confusion across the roadway looking down at their own shattered weapons.

One of them quickly raised a bow and fired an arrow which also glanced off Tom's cloak as easily as the sword and axe blows had. Tom faced them and raised his own sword high above his head and it shot out dozens of fierce dazzling sparks and flares of light in the bright sun, so that the brigands shielded their eyes. Then Jollity flew down in a slow circle and landed on Tom's shoulder. He had hidden the bottle of water in the crook of an oak tree.

'Death to all brigands,' Jollity called out in as loud and scary a voice as he could; it was quite a sound.

The chief brigand stared open-mouthed at the sound coming from the bird on Tom's shoulder. One or two of the other brigands fell to their knees in fear. 'Sorcerer,' the chief brigand was finally able to call out, pointing what was left of his sword at Tom, his face suddenly pale behind the mask of dirt.

Tom walked a step or two nearer the ragged line of brigands and they all took a step back. Tom pointed at his packstaff, bundle, and travel bag where they lay in the road. One of the brigands, already on his knees, picked them up and skittered them all back along the road so that they landed at Tom's feet. Tom hastily stuffed the contents back in while Jollity called out, 'Now go, run away, as fast as you can.'

The brigands wasted no time. They ran off back down the road, as far from Tom and Jollity as they could get.

When the brigands had finally vanished Tom danced a little jig. He kicked up clouds of white dust from the roadway, and as he danced Jollity flew around his head. Tom finally took off the sweltering wolf cape, and held it out in the sunlight.

'That cloak had a powerful magic, all right,' Jollity said.

'It really did, Hafnir was right,' Tom said. He folded it carefully and tucked it neatly back into his travel bag.

'It was almost worth suffering the heat to see the look on their faces when that cloak worked its magic. The best thing of all is that they made me put it on in the first place. I really need to cool down now, though, Jollity,' Tom said.

Tom walked closer to the shaded grass under the circle of broad oak trees. It was certainly cooler among the trees after the hot roadway. He walked in and stood on the grass. He could hear running water from nearby. He could smell flowers too and fresh green herbs. 'Fetch the water bottle back, Jollity,' Tom said, and the bird flew up into a beautiful old oak tree where he had hidden it.

There was a statue of a woman, carved in white marble, on the far side of the tree circle, and Tom went over to it. There were little bundles, wax tablets with pretty wild flowers tied around them and all laid in lines at the statue's feet. Jollity flew over with the bottle and Tom took it and put it back in his packstaff. Jollity flew up and landed on Tom's shoulder.

'A sacred place,' Jollity said, 'by the look of it. These are most likely tributes or offerings to a forest nymph or tree goddess, I should think.'

'I went to a place like this yesterday,' Tom said. 'Dorcon gave me a little parcel just like one of those; it was a poem he had written for a nymph. That's where I filled the bottle. He told me that the water there was very good, and then the oddest thing happened.'

'Go on.'

'An old man, he looked like a hermit, came out from the trees.' Tom looked around nervously in case it should happen here too. 'He said all sorts of odd things.'

'What things, Tom?' said Jollity.

'He said, "That water will do more than quench a

traveller's thirst, it will do more than make you feel better." Then he said, "Beware the labyrinth and the bull. I am an oracle, I foresee all, I tell the future. I have seen the golden giant, the dark king, the ship with black sails." Then he went back again among the leaves.'

'Where was all this?' said Jollity.

'A perfect circle of trees back near where we fought the Cyclops,' said Tom. 'He looked a bit like the forest hermit at home. Home,' Tom said again suddenly, and looked away at the horizon. He had a clear picture in his mind of his mother at home in their neatly painted house near the crossroads to the Land of Stories. She was glancing out of the window at Tom and Big Jack who were walking together up the little path to the front door, and his mother had a big welcoming smile on her face.

Chapter 21

'Where, I wonder, is the honour in all this?' the pirate captain said to himself out loud as he stood on deck. He looked through his spyglass at the approaching shoreline, at the sinister dark island off the starboard bow. His parrot dozed on his shoulder, and for just a moment the captain allowed himself a little daydream about the nice chest of sprite gold doubloons that he would at least be able to haul away from this job as payment: pieces of eight indeed.

Down in the ship's bilge there was an awkward cargo.

Twelve of them altogether, six stroppy and feisty young women, and their six strong young husbands.

The captain's cargo were all sprawled together, locked in their sprite chains.

'I couldn't sleep a wink,' said Jackson mournfully.

'And I thought it was bad being chained up in that flying ship thing,' said Jacquot.

'At least it didn't make you feel sea sick,' said Zinnia.

'No wolves watching us in here,' said Rapunzel.

'I'm not sure if he's not worse,' said Jackie, looking over at the huge pirate guard who was propped up in the doorway, and literally armed to the teeth with a bright dagger in his mouth, crossed bandoliers of bullets across his chest, two flintlocks in his belt, a musket across his knees and a sword in each hand.

'Not much chance of getting out of here, in any case,' said Jack.

'Once we are ashore we'll find a way to escape, my love,' said Jill.

'Arrrhhh mmmmm,' said Sleeping Beauty, yawning and stretching her arms out as best she could in the space, and with the chains.

'Well, at least someone's had a sleep,' said Cinderella crossly.

'Now, now, everybody, we must stay civil,' said Jake. 'It's a good job someone has had a rest. We will need someone to be alert to see what that swine Ormestone has in store for us.'

'I wouldn't mind so much if this boat didn't smell so awful,' said Zinnia, wrinkling up her nose in disgust.

'I suppose I have an advantage there,' said Jill. 'I'm used to it, after all; I spent some years living in a stable.' And she laughed nervously, and a little too loudly, and then so did the others.

'Pipe down, you scum,' said the pirate guard crossly through the dagger in his teeth. 'You'll be laughing on the other side of your faces soon enough when we dock.' He hadn't forgotten how it felt to be hit around the head with a parasol handle.

When the pirate ship docked at the harbour, there were flags flying and a great crowd of excited citizens and townspeople were lined up on the quayside. A throne had been set up on a special platform, and the king sat proudly waiting for the cargo to be unloaded. Ormestone had had a whole new set of robes made for the occasion. He no longer wanted to wear his old fustian black, it seemed wrong in this world of bright sunshine and dazzling blue skies. Instead he had commissioned the palace seamstress, a young girl called Ariadne, to fashion him a whole new outfit. It was made of cloth of gold and gold thread. And so the king sat wearing gold on his golden throne at the top of some golden steps surrounded by gold flags and bunting. He imagined to himself that he made a splendid sight. At the base of his throne were half the pirate crew chained together looking sullen and miserable. They had spent the last few days under a death sentence in a dank dungeon and they weren't happy. There had been another prisoner there too, a fellow wanderer from their own time and place, a decent sort who could tell a good tale at night.

A phalanx of armed guards lined the route from the harbour to the throne. Ormestone was taking no chances, either with the 'cargo', or with the other half of the scruffy gang of pirates who would soon be after their own share of some precious gold. They were all in for what was sometimes called a 'rude awakening'. He smiled to himself at the thought. The drums set up a rhythmic thumping, and then there was a crude fanfare played on the big brass instruments behind the line of guards.

The captain of the guard approached the throne and whispered to the king that, 'the precious cargo, the "catch" had been landed'.

Ormestone soon saw them for himself. They were climbing up the steep pathway, a group of chained figures and a straggle of grotesque armed pirates, and somewhere among them would be his faithful little slave sprite Rumpelstiltskin. How happy he must be, thought Ormestone. Sadly, not for long though, and he smiled to himself. As the group approached Ormestone stood, all resplendent in his gold, raised his arms in what he thought was a kingly fashion and the crowd cheered.

Finally there they were again: the Trueheart brothers all lined up in their chains and shackles.

'Welcome,' Ormestone called out, and so dazzling was he in his gold robes in the bright sunlight that Jake

Trueheart tried to shield his eyes from the sight, only to be pulled up short by the sprite chain at his wrist. Ormestone allowed a sly smile to cross his face. 'Yes, I am a fearful sight in my majesty, am I not?'

'I would say *not*,' said Jack smirking.

'Enough. Welcome indeed to the Land of Myths and Legends. We have brought you here so that you may experience at first hand a real myth in the making, a new story, which will soon be older than time, and you will have a vital part to play in it. Such a privilege.'

'What have you done with our father?' Jacques said. 'If you've harmed him in any way you will have to face us all one by one into eternity, you swine. We will never stop, never give up.'

'Rash words,' said Ormestone. 'Your father is safe for the moment, even as we speak. I rather think it is you who will have to face eternity, especially in the scenario I have planned for you all.' And he allowed himself a regal chuckle.

The pirate captain hopped forward on his crude crutch. His bright parrot looked at Ormestone in all his bright golden splendour and called out, 'Pieces of eight, pieces of eight.'

The Truehearts laughed.

'Beggin' yer kingship's pardon,' the captain said, 'but we 'as done us job as we wuz arsked, and not a true job fer a pirate neither. There is no honour in taking love couples from the happy ever after place. But no matter, just give us our doubloons as was promised, free the rest of my knaves as was also promised and we'll be on our way.'

'I am sorry, I find I cannot spare any doubloons or any other kind of gold from the royal coffers. You are all pirate scum. You came here in the first place thinking you could rob and pillage. By any rights you should all of you be hanging from nooses on these flag-poles,' Ormestone said with glee and then raised his gold-clothed arm.

The armoured guards on either side of the pathway clattered forward with one precise step, their sharp dazzling swords and spears pointing and at the ready. One of the pirates panicked and raised his flintlock pistol. He pointed it at the king. Rumpelstiltskin swiftly raised his own stumpy little arm, held out his rough stick wand, and the gun fell to the ground at once and as it fell it shot another pirate in the foot.

'Ouch,' the pirate cried out, hopping on his one good foot, his own cutlass clattering to the floor.

'Come, lads,' said the pirate captain seeing the hopelessness, 'we's been betrayed, stitched up, done over by a worser pirate even than ourselves ever was. We at least still 'ave our pirates' honour but not this 'un.' And with that he pointed at the king. 'May as well set sail for home and lick our wounds. We may be down, your so-called majesty, but we ain't out. We shall 'ave us a big revenge on yer, you'll see, you mark my words.'

'I think not,' said Ormestone. 'You will never even be able to find this place again. I had you deliberately lured off course with false charts. Guards, release the rest of the scum chained here, then escort them all, both groups, back to their vessel.'

The group of chained pirates were released and the whole furious grumbling gang were led back down to the harbour, while the crowds jeered at them every step of the way.

'I almost miss those pirates now they have gone; perhaps they weren't so bad after all,' said Jack wistfully under his breath.

Chapter 22

King Ormestone was enjoying himself. It was the end of another momentous and busy day. His plans and schemes were all in operation. He had already caused mythic wonders to occur. He had set the Cyclops free to act as a trap, to be a useful early warning system. The one-eyed monster would sniff out any potential and dangerous local heroes in the area, or worse, any brave young Truehearts attempting a rescue.

He had had most of the gold moved now from the official public palace coffers to his own private villa. Now he could look at it, and touch it, as often as he liked, far away from the prying eyes of his guards and captains and all his so-called 'fellow citizens'. He sat now in his spacious ground floor room with the beautiful view of the sea. He was surrounded by as many coins, ingots, vessels, trays, lamps, and gew-gaws as could comfortably be contained in the one room; and all made of the precious sprite gold. He could barely move for piles of gold, and that was just how he liked it. His villa commanded a view of the sea and the island, the very island where all would surely now end for the wretched Truehearts and their silly brides once and for all.

It almost made Ormestone want to laugh to see how pathetically grateful his citizens were that their new king had chosen the twelve new victims from somewhere else other than their own city. Normally the parents in the city would quake in fear every nine years as the time for the lottery came around. Twelve of their young people would be chosen. The fear grew year by year as the time for the sacrifice approached. The old king had tried to devise as fair a method as possible for the selection of the victims. There was no arguing with the result. The fate of the six young men and six young women was sealed and that was that, a certain death in the foul dark tunnels of the labyrinth.

There was a discreet knock on his door.

'Come,' he said importantly, just as a king should.

The door opened and Rumpelstiltskin came in and bowed. 'Your watcher is returned, your majesty.'

The stitched-faced man stood tall behind Rumpelstiltskin. His face was covered by the shadow of a large hood. The stitched-faced man raised his arms and pulled the hood away from his head; his fish-pale skin reflected some of the golden light from the room. He nodded and bowed to his master.

Ormestone ushered them in. He poured himself some wine from a golden jug into a golden goblet, drank deeply and sighed.

'So,' he said, 'you have something to report?'

The stitched-faced man nodded.

'Has someone dared to challenge the Cyclops?'

The stitched-faced man nodded.

'Was it defeated?'

The stitched-faced man nodded again.

'So, who was it? Describe him, what was he like?'

The stitched-faced man held his flattened palm low down near to the ground.

'That, if I may say so, is hardly telling me anything at all. Why Doctor Frankfurter or whatever his name was couldn't have finished you properly and at least stitched a useful second-hand tongue into your mouth, I shall never know. Was it a dwarf, what do you mean?'

The stitched-faced man shook his head.

Then he came forward in a fast lurching walk over to the table close to Ormestone and Ormestone instinctively took a step backwards at the stitched-faced man's huge and threatening approach. The stitched-faced man dipped his long, thick, pale finger into the flagon of wine. He pulled it out again and with his now red, wet finger, he drew a crude heart shape on the white linen cloth that lay folded on the table, and then he nodded again.

'I see, just as I hoped, good,' Ormestone said staring down at the shape on the cloth.

Rumpelstiltskin looked over the edge of the table at the cloth. 'Ah,' he said, 'now I *see*, your majesty. The other Trueheart. The last of the Truehearts has emerged again as the would-be hero.'

'How it is remotely possible that the snivelling little boy Tom Trueheart got here at all, I have no idea, let alone fighting and defeating my fearsome creature,' Ormestone added crossly and in a voice just slightly tinged with fear.

'By trickery, of course, sire, through all sorts of ruses. He is cunning, like all his family,' said Rumpelstiltskin.

'Cunning, cunning, you say; they are just brawny peasant dolts, all of them, as you well know,' said Ormestone.

'Yes, of course, sire, they are indeed all dolts,' said Rumpelstiltskin.

'Where is the poor miserable Cyclops now?' said Ormestone.

The stitched-faced man made a series of gestures at Rumpelstiltskin.

'Back below, chained up again in the gold chamber, nursing his injured eye,' said Rumpelstiltskin.

'Send the watcher away at once,' Ormestone said crossly. 'Tell him to go and do his duty and watch out for the approach of this so-called hero.'

Left alone for a moment, Ormestone looked out over the sea to the fateful island, which loomed darkly on the horizon. 'Well, my little Trueheart, if you want a hero's quest I shall give you one, if you ever dare show your ridiculous little face here.' And he brought his fist down suddenly hard on to the table so that the golden goblet and the golden plates jumped and jangled and the napkin with the red heart stain fell on to the floor.

Part Three
In A Dark Place

Chapter 23

After the incident with the brigands, Tom and Jollity took more care on the road. Tom walked as fast as the heat would allow on the winding roadway. He passed by all sorts of groves and circlets of trees, sometimes oak, sometimes cypress, and all with their white statue or small temple building.

Soon enough Jollity saw the large white marble buildings, the temples and houses of the approaching city. On each building there was a bright golden flag, as if in celebration of something.

Jollity flew back and down and settled on Tom's shoulder. 'The city's just around the next turn of the road, Tom, very big, very bright, and lots of flags out as if there's been, or will be a big occasion.'

'Stay near me, Jollity,' Tom said, fearing now a little for what was just around the corner.

There was a barrier across the road at the edge of the city. Guards in full battle armour and tunics stood on either side of the barrier. Tom couldn't see much of their faces, they were hidden behind the metal guards of their helmets, so he couldn't read their expressions.

They crossed their spears over the barrier as Tom walked up the road towards them.

'Halt, stranger,' one of them called out. 'What is your business here?'

'I am an adventurer,' said Tom, 'come to seek my fortune in the city.'

'By fair means, or foul?' the other guard asked.

'By fair means, of course, sir,' said Tom, 'by honest adventuring.'

'Hmm, you worry me,' said the first guard. 'Where

are you from, boy? Your clothes look wrong, and you are too young to be on the road alone. I am not letting you through until someone in authority has seen you and approves. It would be more than my job's worth to let the wrong person into the city today.'

He muttered something quickly to the other guard who immediately made off at speed up the street. Jollity took off from a near tree branch where he had settled and followed the guard.

Jollity floated on the warm air current above the narrow maze of streets. He watched the guard enter a huge building. Almost at once the guard came out again. A tall broad man was with him, his face hidden by the shaded hood of a cloak, but Jollity recognized him at once as the stitched-faced man, the keeper of the Cyclops and Ormestone's lurching helper from the Land of Dark Stories.

Jollity turned in the air and flew back towards the barrier where Tom stood waiting. Jollity arrived too late. The stitched-faced man had moved faster even than the crow and he arrived at the barrier before Jollity had time to sweep down to warn Tom.

Jollity was forced to hover and watch instead as the

barrier was lifted, and poor Tom taken through under arrest. Then the barrier was lowered, and the two guards moved to stand either side of it again. Tom was led away by the stitched-faced man.

Jollity lifted off from a pole where he had settled and followed as Tom was taken away through the narrow, busy streets of the city.

Chapter 24

King Ormestone had insisted that the decoration of the palace throne room be changed before he would agree to sit in it every day and carry out his duties as king. And so it was changed, and exactly to his orders. The walls were relined with thinly beaten sprite gold leaf of the finest quality. The state furniture was all gilded over too, so that the sunlight dazzled and bounced, and echoed off the walls and the furniture and all round the room. The effect was startling. It was sometimes hard for the various servants and bodyguards to see the king at all, he just seemed to dissolve in the light sitting on his throne right in front of them. Which was just the effect that Ormestone was after; he wanted his own golden presence to dazzle his subjects. The shutters had to be closed on the brightest days just to make sense of everything.

The shutters were half closed on the bright morning that Tom Trueheart was led into the throne room. Even in half-light the room still gave the impression of being made of solid gold all through. Ormestone sat in splendour on his gold throne in his golden robes. He watched Tom's entrance and then he stood to his full height and walked down the steps to greet him. Tom was dazzled by all the golden light, by the aura around the figure of the king in front of him, but not dazzled enough not to know exactly who it was. He too stood up straight to his full height and was unafraid.

'We have met before, young Tom Trueheart,' said Ormestone.

'Yes we have,' said Tom.

'More than once, I should say,' said Ormestone.

'Oh yes,' said Tom, 'we have, sir.'

Ormestone paused to consider the tone of voice that Tom had just used to deliver the word 'sir'. Was he sincere, or was he satirical in intent? Had the boy learned some respect at last, or was he developing just like his wretched brothers and had he become a little more bold, more fearless? It was hard to say. For the moment he let it go.

'That last time I saw you,' he said, 'you were the size of a thumb, I seem to remember.'

There was a quiet chuckle from a small figure who sat on a stool near the throne. Tom recognized the figure at once: it was Rumpelstiltskin. Tom might have known he would be there.

'Yes, sir, your majesty,' said Tom.

And there it was again, that seemingly respectful tone, how to read it?

'And now you have made it all the way across the boundary sea to be here; quite a journey, I would say, for a shrimp like you.'

Tom opened his mouth to speak but Ormestone ploughed on.

'I am told that at long last the weddings of your brothers to their lovely princess brides finally took place as planned.'

Rumpelstiltskin gave a soft little whimper of emotion like a hurt puppy at the words 'princess brides'.

'I hear that it all went off uninterrupted, and that all went swimmingly, and that the brides and their grooms set off for that place, what is it called now? Oh yes, the Isle of Happy Ever After. I am sure they travelled there on great clouds of strewn rose petals, as is the custom at the end of their preferred and feeble stories. A happy ending, I believe it is called. Well, I was not there this time, of course, so I had no way of influencing the outcome. But since arriving here in this place, well, how would we describe the effect of . . . here? Elemental, I think we would call it, either bone chillingly cold, or blood boilingly hot. A place of the fundamentals, the building blocks of stories not just dark, but blood soaked. A place of old gods and old magic. A place of sacrifice and . . . of blood, blood, and more blood.'

He stopped and smiled at Tom with his thin slash of a mouth.

Tom stood, leaning on his packstaff. 'What have you done with my father?' he said quietly.

'What, poor doddery old Daddy? Old Jack the Giant Killer, why he is at this moment in protective custody. Between you and me he hasn't been doing very well at all. For myself I should like to keep him going, but I fear he is past his best, and like a poor faithful old dog it might be better to "relieve" him of his pain, and soon. You look a little sad at the thought, is 'oo going to cwy?' Ormestone added in his horrible mocking baby voice.

With a swift movement of his arm Tom reached down for his birthday sword, only to remember too late that the scabbard, like Mother Hubbard's cupboard, was empty. The guards had taken it, along with the bow and the arrows in his quiver.

'Feisty now, eh, Tom,' Ormestone said almost admiringly. 'You and your family will never learn, it seems. All your weaponry is safely locked away in the palace armoury by now. You disappoint me too, showing your anger like that, young Tom. Surely you understand the necessary rhythms of life: the father is replaced by the sons. It's just a shame that in this case there will be no one to replace him, neither you nor your dozy brothers. I doubt any of you were up to filling his seven-league-boots anyway.'

'I will see you dead yet,' said Tom flatly, calmly.

'Ooh,' said Ormestone, 'ooh, I am frightened now. Mind you, perhaps I should be. I understand that the praise singers and the ballad writers are hailing you as a new hero. You apparently tried to defeat my magnificent Cyclops.'

'*Your* Cyclops?' said Tom, still seething and growing angry at Ormestone's implication that no one would live up to his father and still furious at the loss of his weapons.

'Kept here in this palace, as a guard for the gold and sent out by me to sniff out any possible little heroes like you. Especially you, who might be planning to thwart me, and it worked, you see. I knew you were coming.'

'Thwart you in what?' Tom asked, looking round the bright gold room for a way out, or even a sympathetic face or two? He could only see little Rumpelstiltskin and not far from him a young girl, a little older than himself, standing in a shaft of reflected golden light somewhere behind the throne. She had a nice face and she seemed to be looking at him kindly, though it was hard to tell in all the golden dazzle.

'This, after all, is the Land of Myths and Legends,' said Ormestone, 'a place of wonders. In the north I encountered a dragon with a hoard of sprite gold, and that hoard of gold now sits proudly where it belongs, in my personal villa. My stealing that gold will perhaps have set up a new myth or a legend or two. That brave exploit, that terrible loss. After all, who knows what revenge that dragon will have exacted on those poor cold fools around it? Whatever it is, it will all be sung and rhymed by bearded old bards all over those cold snowy wastes. That gold was all mine and meant to be mine for the taking. From the moment I arrived in that freezing place I managed, without even trying, to mess up the balance. I began a process known as Ragnarok, or "the end of days", the end of everything for them. Quite a glorious result for a once humble story maker, now a Golden King, who likes unhappy endings. Now who will restore their lives back in the cold north, who will end their endless winter? No one from here I am sure.'

'I might,' said Tom.

'You?' Ormestone laughed hard. 'You've never even seen a dragon. I doubt you would last five minutes before it turned you into a roast dinner.'

'No,' said Tom, biting his lip, saying nothing, biding his time.

'This being the Land of Myths and me being who I am, I have a beautiful new story all set out nicely; I think you will enjoy it. Goes like this: imagine if you will a fine little two-masted sailing ship with black sails, mourning sails, the sails of the dead, or about to be dead. Now picture a bleak island not so far from here, and now imagine a giant that guards that island, where lies not only an old king's treasure but also a puzzle, a labyrinth, a maze. Waiting at the centre of that maze another mythic beast, far worse than my Cyclops. Every nine years this beast has demanded a sacrifice from the people here. I have come along and saved this city and their young people and they will all be very grateful to me. Now I have the perfect sacrifice waiting in my dungeons.'

'That's terrible,' Tom said shaking his head. He looked round anxiously for any sign of Jollity at the windows, but it was still too hard to see much in the golden dazzle.

'Oh,' said Ormestone, 'you don't seem very interested in who my chosen sacrificial victims are. That is a shame; I insist that you meet them.' He turned to the guards at either side of the golden throne. 'Fetch the prisoners here at once.'

It was not long before there was the sound of clanking chains and six broad young men and six slender girls were led into the golden room by the guards. Tom didn't turn his head as they were led in. He didn't want to give Ormestone the satisfaction of seeing his possible interest or pity.

Then a familiar voice called out, 'Tom, why, Tom Trueheart, is that you?'

The hairs on the back of Tom's neck stood up in an instant and he felt suddenly very cold. It was, in the old phrase of his mother's, 'as if someone had stepped on his grave,' it gave him goosepimples.

Tom turned his head and saw them all lined up and chained together, stumbling in two lines towards the throne. His brothers Jack, Jackie, Jackson, Jacquot, Jake, and Jacques, and alongside them their wives, Cinderella, Sleeping Beauty, Jill, Princess Zinnia, Snow White, and Rapunzel.

Tom stared open-mouthed; his heart raced, he felt giddy. He had imagined them all this time safely enjoying themselves on the Isle of Happy Ever After, and instead here they were chained and miserable, and once more in Ormestone's power.

'I thought that might quicken your interest, young Tom,' Ormestone said with his nasty cackle of a laugh. 'These fine young people will soon have their own myth to live, never mind any happy endings. Tomorrow they will all travel on the mythic ship with the black sails.'

Ormestone was suddenly interrupted by Rumpelstiltskin. 'All of them, sire?' he said, at once puzzled and fearful.

'Yes, all of them.'

'Surely, your majesty, I thought it was to be just the menfolk,' Rumpelstiltskin added sounding as calm and matter-of-fact as he could, but quivering and seething with emotion inside.

'I don't know where you got that idea, my friend,' Ormestone said quietly, calmly, but with a fierce 'don't mess with me' look on his face. 'In any case,' he added quietly, 'let us not discuss this here, and certainly not now.'

'Yes, sire,' Rumpelstiltskin said, his expression dark, his face suddenly grave.

'As I was saying, they will soon find themselves stumbling around in a strange and confusing labyrinth built a while ago by a king here and designed by citizen Daedalus, I am told; sensible fellow. And there they will meet that very special creature I mentioned before, and after that meeting their myth will be complete. The wonderfully neat thing is that all this only enhances my reputation here. That is because none of these young persons are from local families, so no one will grieve for them and I will be given so much more gold in tribute.'

'I will grieve,' Tom heard Rumpelstiltskin whisper fiercely under his breath, and then Rumpelstiltskin turned and looked directly at Tom. He had a mysterious almost pleading expression on his face and he nodded his head at Tom very slightly, as if sharing a secret with him. Tom was not sure what to make of it.

'Don't listen to that madman, Tom,' Jacques said.

'He's as mad as a box of frogs,' Zinnia said. 'He had us kidnapped from the Island of Happy Ever After.'

'Against all the rules,' added Jill.

'Had us brought here by scurvy pirates, with peg-legs and all,' said Jacquot.

241

'I met a pirate once with a peg-leg,' said Tom, for want of anything better to say.

'Take them all away now,' said Ormestone, anger suddenly clear in his voice. 'Take him too,' he added and pointed at Tom, 'but lock him up well away from the others. I have other plans for him. You disappoint me, young Thomas Trueheart esquire, late of the Land of Stories, I thought we had a bond by now. I thought that my mythic schemes might excite you, but apparently not, you are stuck in your ways. Well, so be it.' Ormestone waved his gold sleeved arm in dismissal. Tom was grabbed by two guards and led away unprotesting. He allowed himself to be taken, and as he was led away in the opposite direction to the others, they called out to him as best they could.

'Don't give up, Tom.'

'Find Dad and defeat that fool Ormestone.'

'Save yourself, Tom.'

'You may well be the last of us, Tom, the last of the Truehearts, and that means the last of all adventurers, ever; just remember that, Tom, and always with a true heart.'

The voices grew fainter as they were all led off further away, until Tom could hear them no more.

Tom was left locked in a smooth stone-walled room with a small barred window. He rattled the bronze door after the guards left, but he knew it would do no good, it was firmly locked. He climbed on to the narrow flat board of a bed and looked out through the bars. He could see a wide expanse of blue sky and the sea glittering in the sunlight, and then some way off on the horizon was the dark outline of an island.

Tom slumped back down on to the hard bed. He wondered where Jollity was and hoped he was all right and that his old friend would soon find him. The time passed, and he thought about his father, also most likely hidden somewhere in here, and all his brothers and their brides too, snatched and brought all the way across the boundary sea by pirates and for what? To be the playthings of mad Ormestone. And what could Tom do about that now? Nothing, nothing at all. He was, after all, just an unarmed small boy locked away in a stone room.

Gradually the light at the window darkened, and looking out Tom could see the wide sweep of the stars. He wondered whether a constellation would ever be named after any of the Truehearts. He slumped back down on to the bed. He was really alone now, his sword and arrows had been taken, and Jollity, it seemed, was lost as well.

Tom would not despair.

Tom would not give up.

Tom was, after all, a Trueheart.

He lay back on the bed, closed his eyes, and tried to sleep. As he was drifting off into a dream of swirling bright stars, he suddenly heard a gentle tap-tapping at the door of his cell.

Chapter 25

OUTSIDE THE PALACE

A FEW HOURS BEFORE

Jollity watched as Tom was marched into the palace by the stitched-faced man. He flew over the building, he flew around it, he hovered in the warm air looking for ways in, for window ledges, for anywhere he might nestle and hide and wait to find Tom. The palace building offered very little. Jollity decided instead to explore the town and the harbour and see if he could find out what Ormestone was up to.

He swept over the narrow streets, swooped past windows; he flew close to people as they watered their potted geraniums, or sat on their sun loggias. There was a sense of something odd around the town, something big was about to happen. Jollity the crow had the sprite sense for such things. He settled for a while fluffing his feathers on various roofs, or on sections of balcony, and marble balustrade. He listened to the people of the city talking about the new king and his plans. They talked in whispers as if they didn't want to be overheard. From what they were all saying he managed to piece together what he thought was due to happen. It was to be soon, the very next morning, in fact. It was something both terrible and shocking, it seemed, and it would involve six young men and six young women and would take place on the island that lay on the horizon. There was to be a blood sacrifice. Something about the numbers involved, six young men and six young women, caused Jollity a worried shiver of recognition, of apprehension, but he dismissed it as impossible.

A blood sacrifice was to take place and for some reason the people of the city were relieved. Gradually Jollity found out why. He heard one woman say, 'Our own sons and daughters at least have been spared.'

Another said, 'It was clever of the king to find those others to take their place, and he was clever to use those filthy pirates to find the new victims. Some justice at last after all the trouble we have had from pirates over the years. It is a good thing to see the tables being turned for once, but still . . . ugh . . .'

Yet another replied, 'I heard he already knew those other young people and he's getting rid of them deliberately. An old grudge, so someone who works at the palace told me. He's mad and cruel that king.'

Pirates, blood sacrifice, an island, a grudge; Jollity was getting confused, he needed to find out more. There was no one he could ask. It was then that he remembered something: Tom and the special water. Tom had met a mysterious old man, someone like the hermit back in the Land of Stories. The man had said he knew the future. He was an oracle. This was just what Jollity needed, an oracle. Tom is unlikely to be going anywhere tonight, he thought, and he set off flying back towards the town where Tom had fought the Cyclops. The waterfall had been somewhere close to that town.

The stars were unusually bright, and Jollity could easily follow the folds and peaks and waters of the landscape as they flowed below him. He soon swept over the small sleeping town with its fine stone houses and central square. He flew lower and circled down across the landscape beyond the town. As he flew so the landscape darkened; the tall dark cypress trees shivered and rustled in the wind. He saw the perfect circle of trees and flew lower.

Jollity landed on a flat stone in the middle of the circle of trees. He closed his eyes and listened hard to all the night noises around him. He used his sprite sense to listen for running water over the noise of all the insects, and owls, and other night-birds. He heard it finally, over the shivering leaves, the croaking frogs, and the brightly chirping cicadas: a faint rushing sound, cooling in the warm night air; falling water.

He followed the noise and then, almost hidden among the rocks, far from the side of the road, he saw it: all silver in the starlight, a small waterfall tumbling into a glassy black pool. He flew towards the water and settled on a branch. Some way in among the tangle of leaves, against the hillside, he saw a blur of warm light. It was a cave beyond the pond behind the falling water almost hidden by branches and leaves. Jollity flew low, skimmed over the water and flew straight into the cave entrance.

There was a tallow lamp burning and against the rock wall sat an old man with a long white beard. He was wrapped in a blanket and a shepherd's crook was across his knees. A small fire barely burned in front of him. It glowed a dull red but gave off little warmth. The old man looked at Jollity as he walked across the cave floor and then he spoke.

'The fire doesn't look much, but it warms my old bones at night,' he said. 'The old hardly sleep, just as we hardly eat. I have seen you before, bird.'

'Have you?' said Jollity, not at all surprised that this noble old man should address him so readily.

'You were bothering the Cyclops and the boy defeated him, a good omen.'

'Yes,' said Jollity.

'You have a question for me.'

'Yes, I have flown from the city. I am confused. In the city they speak of a sacrifice, of young people, twelve in all, and a puzzle, and I am worried for the boy. And more, the king has him prisoner.'

The old man nodded and looked down at Jollity.

'Yes, something is stirring. The new king is fulfilling the regular demand for sacrifice. I shall tell you some of it, not all, because as yet it is mostly un-written.'

'Do you mean that you do not know yet how it will end?'

'Something like that, but not quite. It could go in many directions, stories do. Chances, events, and fate will decide. One thing, perhaps a tiny thing, a wish carried out, a drink of water, the reflection on a shield, a glance into a mirror, the touch of a single finger, might decide the fate of a nation, or even a god. It is like this . . .' The old man settled back against the wall of the grotto, closed his eyes and then spoke.

'On an island, a dark place of shadows, guarded by the giant Talos who is a man made of golden metal, a king once had built, on *my own* advice, a secure labyrinth, a maze of tunnels. At the centre of the maze is the creature, a fearful creature. Born of the cruelty of the gods. It is half man and half bull and it is called the Minotaur. It lurks in its stinking tunnels and demands a sacrifice from the people of the city every nine years. Six young men and six young women must go there to be slaughtered. No one is brave enough to confront and fight the Minotaur. I see a ship with black sails; that is how they will travel to the island.'

'Is there anything that I should do?'

'Find the ship and follow its black wake,' the old man said. His head lolled forwards on to his chest as if he had suddenly fallen asleep.

'Thank you,' Jollity said, but the old man said nothing more to him. Jollity left him asleep in front of the embers of his modest fire, and flew back towards the city.

Chapter 26

Ormestone swept out and away from the throne room after the prisoners were taken away. Rumpelstiltskin trotted after him down the long marble corridor, bobbing in the wake of the golden king.

'Sire,' he said. 'Sorry, *your majesty*,' he added in a pleading voice, 'I am worried that there has been a terrible misunderstanding.'

'No misunderstanding.' Ormestone threw the words back at Rumpelstiltskin without breaking his stride.

'But surely, your majesty,' Rumpelstiltskin continued, 'just the young men were to be sent to the island. Just

252

the young men were to board the ship with the black sails.'

'All are needed for this story to be complete,' said Ormestone, 'all will go.'

'Could we not find others to take the girls' places, your majesty? I was, after all, promised those lovely creatures as my brides once before. To lose them a second time will be a terrible agony for me.'

'Times have changed. I fear then that you will have to suffer your agony. This conversation is at an end. I shall return to my villa to sleep an emperor's sleep in my golden bed. In the morning we shall bid farewell to the Truehearts, every last one of them, and now I know it will be for the last time. I suggest that you get ready to do the same, my old friend, and good night to you.'

'Goodnight, your *majesty*,' Rumpelstiltskin replied quietly, almost under his breath. For Rumpelstiltskin this was a decisive moment. His despair, it seemed, was to be total. He had felt a glimmer of hope and now it was to be snatched away from him. His path was clear.

He had to act; he had waited for too long. His terrible agony, the worst of all things, was stealing up on him so quickly it was close enough to taste. His wand trembled in his hand as a sudden burst of terrifying negative energy rose up in him and threatened to explode outwards. He stood still in the corridor and waited for the feeling to subside.

'Not yet,' he said under his breath, 'bide your time. Not yet, but soon.'

He made his way back through the corridors determined on a new course of action. First he would set Ormestone's victims against him, and then he would turn Ormestone's own desires against himself, which would surely finish him once and for all.

He first went down a long underground corridor. He found his way to the armoury. Inside, a warrior stood guard over the long rows of weapons on the walls. There were thousands of swords, shields, axes, spears, and lances ranged in regimented rows, with everything in its place and a place for everything. This only made Tom Trueheart's sad little pile of weaponry stand out even more. They were piled up on their own, in a bin in the middle of the floor: Tom's birthday sword, dulled and ordinary looking, his arrows, his bow, his packstaff and travel bag. Rumpelstiltskin sighed aloud at the sight of such humble hand-crafted woodland things. They reminded him of that far off cool green forest life in the north, and he sighed again. This time the armoured guard snapped to and saluted him at once.

'I have come for the prisoner's weapons,' Rumpelstiltskin said, pointing at the bin.

'Orders were to keep them here,' said the guard.

'The king himself has ordered me to bring them to him at once,' Rumpelstiltskin said firmly, standing to his full height.

'Perhaps I should just check, and verify the new orders,' the guard said.

'That really won't be necessary,' said Rumpelstiltskin, twitching the twig wand hidden inside his sleeve just a tiny fraction in the direction of the guard, easily numbing the man's mind, lulling him.

'Glad to be of help to his majesty,' the guard said suddenly. 'Sure you can carry it all?'

'Oh, I think I will manage, thank you,' said

Rumpelstiltskin, feeling just a little drained. His sprite powers were strong but he had to save them, conserve the strength of them for when they were really needed. He had never over-used his powers, his sprite magic. Now, however, a different story was emerging, and he would have to use all his powers to the full, even if it meant wearing them out altogether, which was always a danger.

He balanced Tom's things across his arms and set off along the corridor and then down a further, deeper, staircase.

Chapter 27

Tom sat up, wide awake. The tap, tap came again. Tom went to the door. By standing on tiptoe he could just see out through the lock.

The corridor was lit only by small flickering tallow lamps. Tom could just make out a shadow in the gloom. He could not see who it was.

'Hello,' Tom said.

There was no reply, only a click and the singing scrape of metal on metal, and then a louder click, and then a creak of hinges as the door opened slowly inwards.

Tom walked forward and stepped out into the long corridor. He looked around, but there was no one there.

On the stone floor of the corridor were his packstaff, his sword, his arrows, and his travel bag just sitting in a neat little pile in the dim light. He looked up and down, but there was no sign of anyone at all. Tom wasted no time. He picked up his sword and it rippled with bright white light as he tucked it back into its scabbard.

He slipped his travel bag and bow over his shoulder, and put the arrows back into their quiver. He stood straight, breathed in, counted to three in his head, picked up the packstaff and then set off back down the corridor towards a set of stone stairs at the far end.

He knew he had to work his way upwards if he was to find a way out. There were other doors along the low corridor but there was nothing behind them but silence and darkness. There weren't even any guards. It was as if this was the low forgotten end of the palace, a place to which few came. Tom climbed the twisted steps, and another corridor stretched out in front of him. He walked the length of the corridor as quietly as he could in his three-and-a-half-league boots. He headed for the next spiral of stone stairs, but just before he reached them he passed a half open door where a light burned. Tom looked in.

The room was not a cell like his had been; it looked instead like a workroom. There were shelves piled up with bolts of gold-coloured cloth. Two or three tallow lamps burned from the wall, their light reflected from little squares of gold. There was a spinning wheel, and a table covered with a heaped mound of gold cloth. Sitting at the table, with her back to the door, was a young girl with dark hair which shone almost golden in the light. She was bent over the folds of fabric and she was sewing something.

'Hello, miss,' Tom said.

The girl turned round, surprised. Tom recognized her at once as the girl he had seen earlier in the throne room.

'Sorry, I didn't mean to make you jump,' he said.

The girl stood and composed herself. She brushed down her sewing apron, the pockets stuffed with scissors and balls of thread. She pushed the needle she was holding into a pin cushion on the table. 'You're Tom Trueheart,' she said and seemed to be trying not to laugh.

'How did you know my name, miss?'

'I saw you in the throne room. You are the boy with the funny name.' And she broke into a broad grin and laughed a little. 'Sorry, but it is a funny name. You are

259

the boy with the red-heart cloth,' she said pointing to his packstaff, 'the brave young hero who defeated our Cyclops.'

'What are you doing working so late here?'

'I sew for the king, I am the royal seamstress. The king wants more golden robes, more golden cloaks, more golden tunics, more golden everything. Just look at all this golden cloth.' She gestured to the shelves and the bolts of shining cloth piled up to the ceiling. 'How did you escape from the dungeon?' she added. 'I saw them take you away.'

'I don't know what happened,' Tom said. 'There was a knock on the door which woke me up and I saw a shadow, then the door was opened with a key. There was no one there at all when I went out of the door, but all my adventurer's things, my sword and arrows and everything, were all outside the cell on the floor.'

'The gods have smiled on you, Tom Trueheart, because you are brave.'

'I am not brave really,' said Tom.

'You had better shut the door,' the girl said, and she doused each of the lamps, 'in case anyone patrols the corridor; they do that sometimes.'

'I have a lot to do,' said Tom. 'I have to rescue my father and my brothers and their brides, before it's too late. They are all locked away somewhere in here.'

'They are heavily guarded, you could never do it on your own, even though I know you're so brave. You will need help.'

'I have my companion. He is a crow, a bird called Jollity, but I have lost him for now. I am sure to find him again though,' he added doubtfully.

'I don't think that you and a crow would be enough to take on the whole garrison,' the girl said.

'You could help me,' Tom said brightly.

'Well, I could help you escape from the palace,' she looked down at the cloth and the needles, 'and I will,' she said, and a smile lit up her face. 'I am Ariadne,' she added, and made a curtsey with her apron and giggled.

Tom bowed back to her. 'And I, as you know, am Tom Trueheart, of the Adventuring Truehearts and I will rescue you from all this.' He pointed to all the sewing things, and then he hoisted his packstaff. 'Come on,' he said, 'no time to lose.'

'We won't get very far as we are. Once any of the guards see us, and higher up they *will* see us, we'll be done for. Wait, I have an idea,' she said pulling a roll of gold cloth from the table.

They climbed the staircase together up to the next level. Tom was almost completely covered in the golden cloth. At the first sight of any guards Tom was to get into Ariadne's arms and be carried as if he were a golden garment meant for the king. They sped along two more corridors and then turned a corner. Ariadne checked and saw two armed guards either side of the tall doorway that led to the outside. Tom leapt up into Ariadne's arms and stayed as still as he could. Ariadne walked into the corridor.

'Where do you think you are going?' said one of the guards as Ariadne approached them.

'I am taking this new robe to his majesty's villa at once, he needs it for the ceremony tomorrow.'

'Show us it then,' said the other guard, winking at his companion. 'Why not give us a twirl, love.'

'Do you really think that the king would allow me to show this, his newest, most secret golden robe to anyone but himself. Perhaps I should go and ask him if I may show it to you both?'

'Now, we don't want any trouble, dear. My friend didn't mean anything by it; he was teasing you, Miss Ariadne.'

'You may pass,' said the other guard nervously.

'I should think so too,' Ariadne said, and set off through the doors on to the terrace. Tom was already becoming a dead weight in her arms.

One of the guards followed her outside and called after her, 'You won't speak badly of us to the king will you, miss?'

'No. Goodnight,' said Ariadne struggling with Tom's weight balanced across her arms.

'You all right, miss?'

'Yes, I am fine, thank you. Goodnight.'

Ariadne made it to the top of the steps.

'Goodnight, miss.'

It looked a long way down to the shaded streets below the palace and the chance for freedom. A long way and a steep way; the steps swam before her eyes and she almost fell. She righted herself in time and decided it was best not to look down at all.

'That was close. I nearly fell and dropped you. The guards can still see me,' she whispered to Tom. 'I'll do my best to carry you down the first of the stairs.'

She wasn't aware of a pair of dark eyes watching her.

She took a step down and suddenly Tom's weight seemed to lessen, and she took another step, and another, until they were far enough away not to be visible from the palace any more. Ariadne stopped on one of the lower steps and let Tom unfold himself down on to the ground.

'You're stronger than you look,' Tom said.

'I'm not strong at all. It's strange,' she said, 'but you just suddenly felt lighter for a while, I don't know why.'

Neither of them saw the little figure of Rumpelstiltskin as he dashed away back up the steps to the palace.

Tom took the golden cloth from his shoulders, folded it up and tucked it into his travel bag. He and Ariadne set off together through the dark streets under the starlit sky.

As they walked Tom said, 'Ormestone is going to take my brothers and their brides on his so-called mythic ship with black sails. I am going to find the ship and stow away on it and then try and rescue them on the sea or from wherever it is they are being taken.'

'I'll come with you, Tom, if you'll let me,' Ariadne said. 'Let somebody else sew the king's golden robes.'

The harbour was patrolled by more armed guards. Tom could see their plumed helmets bobbing up and down as they walked between the buildings. Tom and Ariadne kept to the shadows as they explored the various wharves and inlets. Finally, at the far end of the harbour arm, they saw the ship with black sails. It was being loaded with weapons, and provision barrels were being rolled up the gangplanks. Tom and Ariadne got as close as they dared and looked for somewhere to hide where they could watch the ship being prepared. There was a narrow passageway between two wharf buildings; it was unlit and just shadowy enough.

They sat together in the warm darkness.

'They are taking your brothers to the island,' Ariadne said.

'What will happen there?' Tom said.

She did not reply for a moment, and there was an awkward silence between them, with just the sound of the creaking timbers of the boat, the gossip of the loads-men, and the shushing sound of the sea.

'What happens there is the worst thing in the world,' she finally said.

'How can that be?' Tom said.

'There is a stone maze, a series of underground tunnels, called a labyrinth, made by a man called Daedalus, and at the centre of it, well, it's as I said.'

'The worst thing in the world?' said Tom.

'Just that,' she said.

They sat together with their backs against the wall and waited for the loading to be finished and their chance to stow away. If Tom craned his neck and looked out between the buildings, he could see the sails unfurled and ready.

Eventually the wharf was quiet. The sailors and loadsmen had gone; just a single guard stood at the base of the walkway. Tom and Ariadne waited. Tom, while keeping an eye on the guard from the shadows, tried to think of a way of distracting him so that they could sneak on board.

Jollity the crow flew low over the harbour area. Various ships of all sizes lay beside the wharves, but there was only one ship with black sails, and it was at the furthest end of the harbour. Jollity flew towards it. He swooped over the ship once or twice and then settled on one of the masts. He folded his wings and looked around. A guard in a plumed helmet stood near the walkway. The buildings were in shadow and there was no one else near that he could see. He stayed still for a few minutes looking into the shadows. A movement caught his eye, as if someone else were also waiting and watching in the dark like him. He concentrated on the gap between two buildings; he was sure that someone was hiding there. He took off silently and allowed himself to glide low between the buildings and down the dark alleyway. There were two figures sitting against a wall. One of them moved his head out to look down the gap and Jollity saw a mass of dark unruly curls, a pale and anxious face, and the hint of a brown leather jerkin. It was Tom Trueheart, for sure, and Jollity's own true heart gave a lurch of fond recognition. He settled quietly close to the two hidden figures.

'Tom,' he whispered.

'Who's that?' Tom answered. 'Is that you, Jollity?'

'Of course,' Jollity said, hopping into view.

'Oh, Jollity,' said Tom, 'I am so glad to see you. This is Ariadne; she helped me to escape from the palace.'

'Hello, Ariadne,' Jollity said.

'An enchanted talking bird,' Ariadne whispered, 'and another funny name.' She suppressed a giggle.

'Ormestone has Jack, Jacques, Jackie, Jackson, Jake, and Jaquot, and Cinderella, Rapunzel, Jill, Snow White, Sleeping Beauty, and Princess Zinnia locked up in his dungeon,' Tom said breathlessly. 'He used pirates to kidnap them from the Isle of Happy Ever After, so now he has them all as well as my poor father.'

'The six young men and six young women,' Jollity said, 'I feared it.'

'They are to be sacrificed,' Ariadne said, 'on the island.'

'I know,' said Jollity.

'You do?' said Tom.

'I found the oracle, the old man at the waterfall, do you remember?'

'Oh him, yes,' said Tom.

'There is another thing,' said Jollity. 'There is a treasure on the island but it is guarded by a metal giant called Talos.'

'And my father is known as Jack the Giant Killer,' said Tom, 'and he killed Ormestone's original giant, so that will be the fate Ormestone has picked out for him. To face another worse giant. We must get on the ship.'

'I am sure we can find a way,' said Jollity. 'I think that a talking bird like me could be quite frightening to a lonely guard in the middle of a dark night, don't you?'

Chapter 28

Ormestone was up and dressed in his finest set of gold clothes. He had hoped for a special new set of robes even more magnificent than the last, but word had been delivered that unfortunately the official palace seamstress, Ariadne, had apparently vanished in the night. Not only that, so had Tom Trueheart. Someone or something had let him out, had released him to cause trouble. Perhaps, he thought, Tom and the little seamstress were in it together. He dismissed the idea. It was all a horrible coincidence and heads would certainly roll for it. The punishment would be swift and severe once he found out who was responsible. It would have to wait now though until later. He had other things to attend to. A severe punishment of the guards responsible could wait a day or so at least. Tom would soon be caught in any case; nothing was to spoil his dark delight, his final triumph over the older Truehearts.

He sat in his golden breakfast room which was filled with dazzling reflections. He had previously ordered that even the fruit was to be gilded—all covered over in thin gold leaf—and there they sat on gold plates. Grapes, pomegranates, figs, apples and pears, too, all burnished and sparking in the sunlight.

It was a perfect morning. He could see the dark island on the horizon and he had a sudden image in his mind of the ending of the story, of the stark terror of the Truehearts somewhere in the dark depths of the labyrinth, and he sighed to himself with pleasure. He ate just the one single grape along with its fine gold covering, and sighed again with another kind of pleasure.

Rumpelstiltskin knocked tentatively at the door.

'Come,' Ormestone said, dabbing flecks of gold leaf from his lips with a gold cloth napkin.

'Good morning, your majesty,' Rumpelstiltskin said, bowing low to the ground.

'I hear,' said Ormestone, 'from those fools of guards that the boy Trueheart has escaped. I suspect that in some way he was let out by the little seamstress, for they have both vanished, and she was to deliver me a fine new gold robe as well. However, I cannot allow such an incident to harm our day of wonders.'

'No indeed, your majesty,' Rumpelstiltskin replied. 'Is it still your wish to send *all* the young persons to the island, including the lovely princesses?'

'Yes, you know full well it is. All of them and of course one other. The pathetic father, he is to be dispatched too. He was famed as a giant killer; as I remember it, he killed one of my first great creations. Well, let's see how he fares against another giant. It will be the last for him, the very giant of giants, completely undefeatable.' And he laughed his unpleasant laugh.

'Do you mean the Cyclops from the cellar, sire, your majesty?' said Rumpelstiltskin.

'No, think for a moment. A far worse giant awaits any warrior who ventutres on to the island over there, and in the unlikely event of him beating that giant too, well, it just opens up the old king's treasure for us just that bit earlier.'

'Ah yes,' said Rumpelstiltskin, 'of course, so it does.'

'I have been thinking,' Ormestone added quietly, 'you are in a position to grant almost anything that your sprite magic encompasses?'

'True, your majesty, within reason.'

'I know that you have not, and will not, make sprite gold directly for me, but might you grant me the power to make my *own* gold, perhaps, at a touch. I shall need huge amounts of gold if I am to achieve my dream of changing the whole course of Myths and Legends.'

'I am not sure, your highness,' Rumpelstiltskin said quietly. 'It would be a very powerful enchantment to grant,' he added, a plan forming suddenly and clearly in his head. 'Perhaps after today's excitements, your majesty, I might try it, but I cannot promise it would work.'

'You will make it work, I am sure,' Ormestone said, almost beside himself with excitement.

Chapter 29

The Trueheart brothers and their brides were led in chains out of the palace dungeons and up into the bright early morning sunshine. Their chained arms were held straight down at their sides; their feet were set slightly apart. They looked like a batch of very scruffy, unsuitable new recruits for the king's army. A long line of guards in plumed helms lined every side of the square courtyard.

The king himself was already rushing through the lower dungeon corridors with two strong soldiers. He looked like a bolt of the Cyclops's lightning, as his gold cape flashed around the walls in all the gloom and darkness. He heard the welcome but threatening growl of one of his pet guard lions. He was soon at the cell. Big Jack sat against the wall, the sprite chain loose on the filthy floor.

'Well,' Ormestone snapped to Big Jack, 'your time is up. My patience has finally worn away to nothing. Your usefulness to me is at an end. We are taking you now, today, across the sea to face something truly terrible. You and the rest of your benighted family shall bother me no more. You will fade into myth. Guards, take him with the others.'

The king's guard entered the cell, bristling with swords and spears. Big Jack stood and then deliberately patted the angry looking guard lion on the head so that its hackles rose. It pulled on its leash and it roared and snapped angrily. Its fearsome anger distracted everyone just enough for Jack to be able to slip a bag of dark powder from the wall cavity into his breeches pocket.

Jack was finally pulled out blinking into the bright sunlight. Six of his sons were lined up in chains, and alongside them he could see their six beautiful brides. A great cry went up and the six young men strained forward in fury on their chains. Jack looked across at his sons, but pull as he might on the sprite chain he could not get near them. And they, though they tugged and pulled and wrenched at their own chains, could not get near him.

'I will save you, my boys,' he called out, while being pushed along by the soldiers.

'No,' Jake shouted back, 'fear not, father, we will save you.'

The king bustled out into the courtyard. 'No one will save anybody,' he cried out, and laughed his cackling laugh. The brothers responded with a chorus of shouts and boos so that the guards were forced to pull them all back into line and hold swords to their throats to silence them.

The king stood in all his dazzling gold. Rumpelstiltskin stood behind him looking hot and bothered in his crown of leaves and his leather tunic. Rumpelstiltskin walked up to the line of the princess brides and as he walked past each one he looked pityingly up into their beautiful faces. But they seemed to pay no attention to him, they were too busy looking over at the slumped, seemingly broken figure of Big Jack.

'I am sorry,' Rumpelstiltskin whispered to each of the girls in turn, even Jill, and he said it as quietly as he could, so that the king should not overhear him.

The girls just shook their heads and ignored him.

King Ormestone mounted his golden platform and surveyed the scene. A golden carpet had been laid to the steps and beyond, all the way down to the harbour and the bright blue sea. From where he stood he could see the ship with the black sails bobbing on the tide as it waited for its precious cargo.

'Soon,' he began, addressing the Truehearts, 'we will travel to the island where the fates will decide your ends once and for all. This will not be a happy ever after kind of island. No, far from it, rather this will be an island of darkness and blood and fear. It is, I am afraid, by all accounts, a truly terrible place. Perhaps the dark gods will be merciful, but I doubt they will be. The only one missing is your pathetic brother young Tom Trueheart. He escaped with a little girl; he has run away with her to pick buttercups and daisies somewhere and has left you all to your fates. I think that shows his character clearly enough. Come, guards, take them to the ship.'

'Wait,' Big Jack called out in a big voice. He shuffled forward, straining against the chains across his ankles. 'You should know something about my boy, young Tom. I was the seventh son of my father, and he is my seventh son, that makes him the seventh son, of a seventh son. He is capable of more than *you* can ever know.'

'Your pathetic little backwoods superstitions and

beliefs will not affect me here,' said Ormestone, his lip curled in disgust. 'This is the place of real fundamentals,' he added. He raised his gold-sleeved arms and the guards set to and marched the prisoners off in a long line towards the harbour. As they moved away no one paid any attention to the crow that took off from the top of one of the many flagpoles and followed the line of soldiers and prisoners through the town.

Chapter 30

THE SHIP WITH BLACK SAILS

NIGHT TIME

Tom and Ariadne waited while Jollity flew across to the ship with the black sails. Just the one palace guard stood at the end of the ramp leading up to the deck. To Jollity the guard looked half asleep; he did not think it would take much to spook him. He flew silently above the guard and settled on the rail above the deck and then he spoke as loudly as he could.

'The oracle speaks,' Jollity said, using the voice that had spooked the brigands on the road.

The guard spun round and drew his sword, but he could see no one, just the darkness of the empty harbourside.

Jollity spoke again. 'The oracle speaks to you, yes, you there; you must leave this place now and never return.' Jollity's frightening voice echoed from the walls, and rang around the harbour.

The guard ran to one side, to where he thought the voice had come from, his sword raised in his hand. 'Come out and show yourself,' he called out. There was no sign of anyone, just empty darkness. The guard ran to the other side, swiping his sword through the empty air wildly.

'You missed me,' Jollity called out, 'and look, you missed me again; you will always miss. You cannot defeat . . . the unseen.'

Tom and Ariadne watched from the shadows as the guard raced wildly to and fro. Jollity lifted a little pottery lamp from a pile of them on the deck of the ship. He held it in his beak. He flew silently and suddenly dropped the lamp behind the guard so that it smashed on the ground. The guard leapt in the air as if he had been struck. Jollity had already flown back and fetched another of the ship's lamps. He flew just as silently and dropped the other lamp close behind the first. The guard leapt up in the air again. Tom had to cover his mouth to keep from bursting out laughing, the guard looked so silly.

'Leave now,' Jollity quavered, 'for death is coming to all on the black-sailed ship and that means you too.'

The guard looked down at the scattered pottery fragments around him, stared into the darkness at nothing, and then ran away from the gangplank and the harbour back in the direction of the city.

Tom took Ariadne by the hand. They crouched and ran quickly up the gangplank on to the deck. They needed a hiding place. There were six big empty barrels on the deck, and Tom had a horrible idea of what use they might be put to after the visit to the terrible island.

They climbed in and sat hunched up together at the bottom of a barrel that smelt of sour wine lees.

During the night they talked quietly together. Tom told Ariadne about life in the Land of Stories; he told her the stories of his brothers and their brides. She told him about the world she lived in, the Land of Myths and Legends. They sat pressed against the side of the barrel while they waited for the sunrise.

Eventually the sky faded into a disc of flawless blue above the barrel opening. They heard marching feet and banging drums, and the brass fanfares of the approaching king. Soon enough those same feet were stamping on the deck of the ship close to their barrel. Tom could not risk taking a look, but he could hear the rattle of chains, and imagined his brothers all lined up. There was movement as the ship cast off from the dock and the sudden cheer of a great crowd of people.

'They are happy because none of their children are going to that island,' Ariadne whispered.

Tom looked inside his travel bag and found the remaining piece of the square of Trueheart cotton that his father had left inside the wooden bowl at Uhn's house in the far off cold north.

He threw the piece gently up and out of the barrel opening, and he saw it caught by the sea breeze and lifted away.

The fragment of cloth drifted in the air and then fell to the deck where the wind took it and blew it across the wooden boards until it ended up against Big Jack's seven-league boot. Big Jack noticed it at once, lifted his boot and brought it down to cover the cloth.

He knew exactly where he had left it, and he smiled just slightly at the thought that Tom had found it, had picked up on his clue and was even now somewhere improbably near. There could be no doubt now that the Truehearts would soon be ready to fight back.

Big Jack stood at the end of the line of Truehearts. The sprite chains that bound them were linked together and joined to the mast. Some way above them on the cross spar, part hidden by the movement of the black canvas sail, sat a single black crow watching everything that was going on with a beady eye.

King Ormestone and Rumpelstiltskin stood in the prow of the ship watching the island grow larger and closer with every breath of hot wind. Rumpelstiltskin stole a glance every now and then at his beautiful princesses standing so proud and defiant, swaying with the motion of the ship. Soldiers were lined up on board too and even Ormestone's guard wolf was keeping a close eye on Big Jack. The Trueheart men were restless, struggling against the chains, despite the threat of the guards' swords every time they did so.

The self-styled King Ormestone turned from the prow and addressed them all.

'My wish is about to come true. I have arranged the perfect dark ending for you all. I will see you put into the labyrinth, and after that no one will ever see any of you ever again.'

'What labyrinth?' Jake called out defiantly. 'When we are free then you will be the first to suffer.'

'You are wrong, my ignorant young friend. The first to suffer will be your father, old Jack the Giant Killer himself. He killed one of my first creations, a fine giant, and he will be rewarded for it in the best way I can imagine, and in a very few minutes, as you will soon see.'

Big Jack was tempted to laugh out loud, but he said nothing; he retained his dignity, staying as still as a rock, betraying nothing.

The brothers were in immediate uproar. They surged forward against the chains. It took all the guards, and all the guards' strength, to hold them back.

'We told you what would happen if you hurt our father,' they shouted.

Tom listened, fearful and angry, inside the barrel.

'When there's a chance,' Ariadne said, 'we will escape and do what we can.'

Then a sailor called out, 'Land ahoy, heave to.'

Chapter 31

ON THE DARK SHORE

A MEETING WITH A GIANT

11.13 A.M.

The ship was anchored in the shallows and while the crew fussed with ropes and chains and the sails, Jollity lifted off from his spar and flew with slow, quiet beats of his wings over to the island itself. He soared upwards once clear of the ship and flew inland.

The island was made of what looked like harsh grey volcanic rock; there were patches of rough green grass, but the sand was black. It looked like an arena created for death. What an awful place to die, Jollity thought, looking at the bleak shore below. There was a central wall made of grey stone which rose sheer into the air and it made a square with a tall tower on one side and a dark, covered entrance way. Jollity flew over, landed on the tower and looked back at the ship.

There was already a little procession. Two guards and Big Jack Trueheart were walking over the black sand in the shallows towards the shoreline. Jollity heard a trumpet fanfare from the ship. This was followed by a strange unearthly noise that set his nerves on edge. It was a metallic creaking and a terrible high pitched squealing. It sounded as if two huge dry metal surfaces were straining and grinding against one another. Then at once there was a thump like a huge bass drum being struck with a hammer, and then another. Jollity the crow turned his head and saw something towering over him, something so terrifying that he nearly fell off his perch. 'Oh no,' he whispered.

Moments before, on board ship, Ormestone had ordered Big Jack's chains to be struck. Rumpelstiltskin pointed his wand and the sprite chain slithered back into itself, leaving Big Jack free.

'Remind me,' Ormestone said, 'what was your name all those years ago back in the Land of Stories?'

Jack stayed silent. He glared back at Ormestone, unblinking, then he stretched up and then bent forward and casually adjusted his boot top, taking the chance to slip the little fragment of Trueheart cloth out and tuck it into his boot. He straightened and said calmly, defiantly, 'I was renowned as Jack the Giant Killer, as you well know.' A great cheer went up from the Trueheart boys.

'I am told,' said Ormestone, 'that on this island there is a mythic giant. He is the giant of giants, and he is called Talos. He is a man made of gold metal, a fierce brass warrior. Time for you to face him, Jack Trueheart, and die before the rest of your family are thrown into the labyrinth for ever. At least I have offered you a heroic death, out in the open under heaven, not in the darkness and filth of an underground Hades.'

Big Jack said nothing.

'Typical,' said Ormestone. 'You two escort him ashore and then leave him to fate.'

The guards, with Big Jack between them, clambered down the side of the vessel. They walked through the surf and up on to the black sand, and then Ormestone signalled the fanfare. The trumpet blew its note which soared and echoed round the island, and through the twisted tunnels, the maze of the labyrinth, right into the dark heart where a hungry and shadowy beast stirred from a long sleep.

Then came the strange metallic screeching noises and Talos the giant suddenly walked into view. The two guards on the beach dropped back at the sight of him, their mouths slack. They turned and scrambled back through the surf to the ship.

The brass fanfares fell silent. Even Ormestone was stunned into silence. All eyes were on the towering metal giant.

Tom looked out of the barrel lip, and noted the sudden distraction. 'Come on,' he whispered, 'now's our chance.' Ariadne climbed out after Tom and they slipped over the side of the ship into the shallow water.

They waded around the hull of the ship and up through the surf on to the beach, sheltered by the bulk of the ship.

There was very little cover once on the beach. The black sand was punctuated by clumps of grey rocks, some scrubby sea grass, a stretch of more black sand and then the looming grey stone wall. Tom and

Ariadne crouched and ran up the beach to the rocks and ducked down behind them. Tom finally got a proper look at Talos. He stood towering over the strange wall that ran across the island.

'Oh no,' Tom said. 'Look at that; even Big Jack surely can't defeat that.'

Ariadne said, 'By Zeus, that monster will kill us all. He guards the old king's treasure here on the island. I heard them talking at the palace.'

Talos stood sixty or more feet into the air. His huge body was made of shining gold metal. You could see at once that it wasn't real gold though, because it was tarnished and pitted with verdigris. There were stains and streaks of dark water damage around his joints. He held a huge shining sword in one hand and a spear in the other and he swayed slightly on his legs. He studied Big Jack who was now left alone and exposed on the black sand facing Talos down. The giant was still, blocking out the sunlight, casting a deep shadow across Big Jack. Then Talos moved his sword arm up, with a squeal of metal scraping on metal.

Big Jack had no weapons; he stared back at the giant trying to make sense of his huge body.

Big Jack ran across the sand to the side of Talos, and Talos brought his sword arm down fast. The sword missed Jack and landed on the ground, lifting a great cloud of black sand up into the air. Jack ran further up the beach and the giant turned and followed him. It covered a huge distance with just one stride and was already ahead of Jack when the sword was brought down again in front of him with devastating speed. This time the sword struck a formation of sharp looking volcanic rocks which shattered and sent showers of sparks up into the air, as well as shards of rock. Tom and Ariadne ran out from behind the ruined rocks.

'Tom,' Big Jack called out. 'My dear boy, I am glad to see you again, lad. Careful, watch yourselves, he's a big one.'

The golden spear landed in the sand between them with a huge thud. Tom pulled Ariadne out of range of the spear blade. Then Tom took his sword from the scabbard and a great burst of reflected light blazed out from it.

'Fine sword, lad,' Jack said diving to the ground. 'Wonder who made that for you?' And he rolled quickly across the sand as the giant's sword was brought down again with a huge crash between them.

'Wave your sword around, distract him,' Jack called out.

Tom ran down the beach with his own sword raised high, sending back bright shattering beams of light at the giant. Talos shook his great metal head as if he had been dazzled and then took a shaky step forward towards Tom, and Tom edged backwards fast, while Ariadne took her chance and ran off towards the covered entrance way in the huge wall.

'That's it, Tom, good work,' Jack called out, and he suddenly leapt up from the ground and grabbed hold of the giant's metal leg and began to climb it. Talos seemed unaware of Jack clinging on to his leg and he strode forward regardless, straight at Tom.

Tom dodged nimbly from side to side as the sword came down this way and that, gouging out great tracts of black sand and rock. Tom managed to stay just one leap ahead.

Jack was clutching on to the giant's thigh with one arm. With the other he fished out a small cotton bag from his breeches pocket. He undid the fastened end with his teeth, and tipped some black powder into the giant knee joint. Then with the bag held in his mouth Jack leapt across and landed on the other leg and tipped some more of the black powder in the other knee section. He climbed higher up the shining body trailing the black powder around and into the waistband on the giant's sculpted metal tunic. Then went higher still around his great neck. Finally Big Jack put the remaining bag full of powder down into the gap between the sword handle and the jointed brass fingers.

Then Jack jumped away from the sword arm, clung on to the folds in the giant's brass tunic, slithered back all the way down the metal body, and then he slid down a leg until he was on the ground again. Jack rolled over and over across the sand and one of Talos's huge metal feet squealed and slammed into the soft ground only inches from Jack's head. Tom was still jumping around, zigzagging and waving the bright sword to distract Talos.

Jack called out to Tom. 'Tom, over here fast.'

Tom dodged through the giant's legs as Jack jumped up and then shouted, 'Over to the wall, Tom.' They both ran across the beach towards the looming doorway. Tom could see Jollity sitting perched up on the tower and Ariadne was already hidden in the shadow of the doorway. Talos turned with an extra loud squeal and screech of twisting metal, and took a step towards them.

'How are you with the bow, Tom?' Jack asked.

'Not bad,' said Tom breathlessly.

Talos towered over the wall and sliced the sword at the tower and Jollity flew up into the sky. Great lumps of stone crashed around Tom and Big Jack. Tom took an arrow from his quiver. Big Jack pulled out the little remaining section of Trueheart cloth from his boot where he had stuffed it.

'I can't tell you how glad I was to see this little bit of Trueheart rag back again, Tom. The success of this idea all depends now on you having packed some tinder,' Big Jack shouted over the noise of Talos. Tom rummaged in his travel bag, and like Little Jack Horner he pulled out a plum, his tinder kit.

'Good boy,' said Big Jack.

'Cicero made me pack it,' Tom said.

'Good old Cicero, he always knows what's what.'

The giant's spear head suddenly split the ground between them and quivered there for a brief moment before it was hauled out again.

Jack quickly tied the heart cloth near the arrow head end of the shaft.

'I have done this before,' Tom shouted. 'I vanquished the Cyclops the same way.'

'Good thinking, lad,' said Big Jack, and then he pulled a tiny silver bottle out of his pocket, unstoppered it and splashed the contents on to the heart cloth.

'Light it now, Tom,' he said urgently.

Tom fussed with the tinder, aware of the shadow of Talos above them, of the grinding screech as his sword arm came down again and again, narrowly missing Big Jack. The sparks kept being blown by the wind in the wrong direction. Talos lifted his sword high above his head. The sparks finally drifted on to the heart cloth and the cloth burst into flame.

'Now, Tom,' said Big Jack.

Tom stepped out of the shelter of the doorway; he raised the bow and arrow to his shoulder.

'Aim for the sword hand,' Big Jack said.

Tom took careful aim and loosed his flaming arrow.

Chapter 32

Ormestone stood, gold and resplendent, on the deck of the ship. He ordered the Truehearts and their brides to be unchained and held ready. They stood together unable to see what was happening on the beach, but they kept up their low mutterings and threats. Ormestone ignored them for now; the soldiers had them pinned down in any case. He waited for Talos to discover Big Jack. He did not have to wait long. The huge metal creature soon strode into view, sword and spear at the ready.

Big Jack's guards on the beach turned tail and fled

at the sight of the golden metal giant striding towards them across the black sand.

'Fools,' Ormestone said to Rumpelstiltskin. 'That's two more for punishment.'

'Oh yes, sire, your majesty,' Rumpelstiltskin said.

'A magnificent sight though, is he not?' Ormestone said.

'Indeed he is, your majesty.'

'Imagine if that giant were made of solid gold,' Ormestone added dreamily.

'That would be quite something to see,' Rumpelstiltskin replied.

However, Ormestone's dreamy pleasure turned to violent anger when he saw Tom and Ariadne suddenly scuttle up on to the beach. He pointed his gold-sleeved arm out across the water.

'Where did they come from, and where did he get his weapons?'

'I cannot imagine, your highness,' said Rumpelstiltskin.

'Treachery, that's what it is, treachery,' Ormestone seethed.

'They are only children, your majesty,' Rumpel-stiltskin said. 'They can hardly harm that magnificent thing.'

'I hope you're right.'

As the skirmish unfolded on the dark beach in front of them, Ormestone got more and more angry. He readied his guards for an all-out assault just in case the giant Talos should fall. And then Tom stepped out and raised his bow.

Chapter 33

Tom took as careful an aim at the giant's sword hand as he could. He allowed for the hot wind and the distance, and the fact that the sword arm was about to fall. He couldn't take too long, the sword arm was at its zenith, and the flames on the arrow shaft would soon burn through the cloth and the arrow shaft itself. Besides Tom was out in the open and vulnerable to the terrible sword. He fired. The flaming arrow arced upwards towards Talos the giant. It dipped at just the right moment as the giant brass arm came down, so the arrow flew straight into the dark gap where his metal fingers gripped the sword. There was a sudden flare of light. A light even brighter than the reflected dazzle of sun on the golden metal skin of the giant. The light travelled all over the giant's body in a split second—a streak of yellow gold lightning, as if the Cyclops itself had thrown it. The giant's arm froze in mid swipe and then there was an enormous explosion as the black powder caught and the giant Talos was blasted into huge fragments. His sword hand, still holding the sword, flew up high and turned over and over in the air. The giant's massive body and the spear arm blew apart and chased each other across the black beach, bouncing and crashing against the rocks until finally splashing into the sea. The giant's legs stayed upright for a moment and then they crashed forwards across the sand. Finally, the giant's enormous head, with its two blank and staring eyes, suddenly landed with a huge thump in the black sand right in front of Tom and Big Jack.

There was a great cry from the ship. It was Ormestone. He stood in the prow shaking with fury. He ordered all the troops ashore at once. The first wave of soldiers splashed through the water and ran warily towards the beach.

'I must tell you something, Dad.'

'Be quick, they are on their way.'

'I am sure that it was Rumpelstiltskin who let me out of my cell and gave me back my weapons.'

'The devil you say. Good for him, could be useful. Now run, Tom,' said Big Jack. 'Don't think about it, keep yourself in reserve, don't get caught, just run and take young Ariadne with you.'

'But, Dad—' Tom started.

'But me no buts, Tom,' Big Jack interrupted. 'Do as your father tells you. There, that's a first, eh, Tom? Now run like the wind, the both of you. I'll manage fine. Those pirates that he locked up in my cell with me were very obliging fellows, they taught me some useful stuff as you have already seen. Now, off you go, and Tom . . . '

'Yes, Dad?'

'With a true heart though, eh, lad?'

'Of course, always that, Dad, always. I'll be right behind you,' Tom called back as he grabbed Ariadne and they ran off together. They skirted the huge, blankly staring head of Talos, ran up beside the towering wall, and carried on running, hand in hand.

Ormestone arrived on the black shore surrounded by his armoured soldiers. Tom watched, safely hidden behind part of the wall, as his father was taken and lined up next to his own sons and their wives. They stretched out along the beach among the fallen chunks of Talos.

'Well, Big Jack,' said Ormestone, 'it seems we have lost your youngest, that little baby coward Tom, but no matter, when we leave this place he will just have to stay here for ever and rot, there will be no way back across the water for him. We have reached the end of our adventures together. You have destroyed yet another noble giant; it seems you are correctly named after all. It is a shame that no one in our futures will ever read of that particular triumph. You will soon be devoured, along with your sons and their hapless wives. My men will take you into this place and they will leave you there.' He gestured up at the huge wall and the doors. 'No one ever comes back from inside there. All your cunning and courage will be as nothing when you are face to face with what lurks in those passages.'

His words carried up the beach to Tom and Ariadne.

'I will go in after them somehow. I have to try,' said Tom.

'I know, Tom, that's what I'm afraid of,' said Ariadne, fearfully.

The soldiers pushed the protesting and noisy chained group of adventurers and brides towards the doors of the labyrinth. Rumpelstiltskin stood still, transfixed where he was on the black sand, the sea water pooling around his boots. His beloved princesses were being bundled away from him. It was the last he would see of them, ever. He could not allow this to happen, but there were too many loyal, well paid, and bribed soldiers between him and them. Even if he used his sprite magic he could not tackle them all at once. He ran up the beach; perhaps he could do one thing at least. He drew level with the group, his twig wand in his sleeve.

Jackson saw him peeping round one of the soldiers. 'I see you've brought your pet rat with you,' he shouted at Ormestone.

'Poor old Rumply,' said Princess Zinnia, 'he really loves us all, you know.'

Rumpelstiltskin closed his eyes and intoned some words, mumbling them quietly under his breath.

The soldiers heaved the great doors of the labyrinth open, while Rumpelstiltskin pointed his sleeve at the struggling group.

The huge bronze doors swung outwards finally, revealing a solidly black entrance way. A cloud of greenish smoke drifted and dispersed out into the air, and along with it came a terrible smell of old rotten meat.

'Take them inside,' Ormestone shouted covering his slash of a mouth with his fine golden sleeve.

The soldiers pushed the group into the dark space beyond the doors, prodding at them with swords and spears, pushing them into the darkness. The group, being chained together, stumbled awkwardly and then fell as they were pushed further into the darkness, and then there was a great roaring noise from somewhere among the stinking tunnels.

'Ah,' cried Ormestone, 'I hear the beast; he smells his dinner. It has been a long wait for him. He will find you all, fear not, you cannot hide from him. We shall never see each other again. Your stories are finished and all your future stories too. You will never live now to carry them out. Poor old Big Jack can't save any of you, let alone himself. Farewell, let us hope you can all die with some dignity.'

'You'll never get away with this,' Jackson called out. 'We will—' He got no further. The beast roared again and the sound drowned his words.

'Push them over the edge, shut and lock the doors,' Ormestone interrupted, with a wave of his arm.

The soldiers moved in a line, spears and swords

forward. They pushed the prisoners back. Ormestone clearly saw the chains fall away from the arms and legs of the princesses, then the soldiers pushed everyone over the edge and they all vanished with a cry, into the further deep darkness. The soldiers withdrew. The doors clanged shut, one of the soldiers turned the huge bronze key, and there was a sudden silence, broken only by the sound of the sea on the black shore.

'Throw away that key at once and as far as you can,' Ormestone said to the soldiers. The key was thrown high and far. It finally landed deep among some prickly bushes, with a clunk. A black crow bird sitting high up on the top of the building saw exactly where it fell and quietly took off.

'Arrest him,' Ormestone said and pointed at Rumpelstiltskin, 'and make sure you take his little wand,' he added. Rumpelstiltskin was surrounded at once by armed guards. 'Take him to the ship,' Ormestone said quietly.

'But, your majesty,' Rumpelstiltskin protested, 'I have done nothing but help you.'

'I saw what happened just now,' Ormestone said, 'you freed those girls, you loosed their chains, just before they were pushed down into the labyrinth, I saw it all happen.'

'What about the treasure, sire?' Rumpelstiltskin pleaded, desperately changing the subject.

'With what you are going to grant me, I will no longer need to plunder any ancient treasure. To the ship now, and hurry.'

Ormestone and the line of soldiers marched little Rumpelstiltskin down the beach, back to the ship with the black sails. Tom watched as it sailed away. Jollity suddenly flew down next to Tom, and dropped the key out of his beak at Tom's feet.

'Here you are, Tom,' he said, 'I think you will need this. Nothing I can say will stop you from going into that terrible place will it?'

'No,' said Tom.

'You heard that noise, Tom, from in there,' said Ariadne. 'It was awful, it made my flesh creep.' She shivered. 'And how will we ever get back again across the sea to the city?'

'I have to go in there, Ariadne,' said Tom. 'We can worry about getting back later. My first job as a Trueheart is to rescue my family.'

'You're sounding more and more like an adventurer, Tom,' said Jollity.

'No,' said Tom, turning to Jollity and picking up the bronze key, 'I am sounding more and more like a Trueheart. Come on.' And he stood up and ran down the slope towards the gate with the key in his hand.

'Wait for me, Tom,' said Ariadne hurrying behind him.

Chapter 34

IN THE LABYRINTH

It took both Tom and Ariadne, pulling hard together, to open the bronze doors. The terrible rotten smell wafted out around them.

'Carrion,' said Jollity, nodding his head.

Tom drew his sword. It flared with light and they were able to see into the darkness.

'Dad,' Tom called out. His voice echoed around the stone walls. The only reply came from somewhere below, a very distant scream which echoed up and around the walls.

'I'm going down there,' Tom said.

Jollity landed on his shoulder. 'I'm coming too.'

'So am I then,' said Ariadne.

'No,' said Tom, 'no, please, Ariadne, this is my battle. I must rescue the Truehearts, it is my story, my destiny. I really don't want you to get hurt, Miss Ariadne, you've done so much already to help. You must stay here safely. We may need your help later, if we get through this, that is. Why, anything could happen.'

'The labyrinth is a maze of corridors. You will get lost, you may never find your way back,' Ariadne said.

'I'll work something out,' said Tom doubtfully.

'Wait,' said Ariadne, 'I have an idea.'

She reached into the pocket on her tunic, and pulled out a spool of the gold thread she had been sewing with in the little cell when Tom first met her.

'If we tie this end of the thread here on the door lock,' said Ariadne, 'then you can unwind it as you walk and then just follow it back here, when . . . '

'When what?' said Tom.

'When you have . . . finished,' said Ariadne quietly. A silence fell then between all three as Ariadne tied the thin thread to the huge door handle. Tom took the spool and walked forward to the ledge while the thread trailed out behind him.

'It works, Tom,' said Jollity.

'Good,' said Tom, but it didn't sound as if there was anything good about it from the way that Tom spoke, it sounded anything but. Another scream and a following roar echoed up from the maze of corridors below them.

'Right,' said Tom swallowing hard. 'Come on then, Jollity.'

'Good luck, Tom,' said Ariadne, and she held out her hand. Tom took it.

'See you very soon,' he said, 'I promise.'

'I hope so, Tom, I really do.'

Tom walked to the back of the entrance space. A ridge ran along the back wall and below the ridge a walkway descended into the darkness. This was where his brothers, their brides, and his father had been pushed over at sword and spear point. Jollity flew down into the dark while Tom held his sword up to light the spiral ramp.

'Nothing so far,' Jollity called out. Tom jumped over the ridge, landed on the ramp, and walked downwards into the darkness.

Chapter 35

Tom made his way down the ramp, holding his sword high, lighting the way. The further he went, the further he went into the darkness and heat and the awful stale meaty stink and the less the light glowed from his sword. He could hear the noises now too, the confused voices of his family, and the grunts and roars of something else. Jollity flew back suddenly and landed on his shoulder.

'It's a puzzle of a place down there, Tom. Nothing makes any sense. I can hear them but I can't find them. I fly to where I think the noise is coming from and there is another twist and another and then endless awful darkness. I have never seen anything more dark. You will have to be very careful down there, Tom.'

The sword still gave out enough light to see the turns and angles of the high stone walls which made up the maze. Tom kept turning to the left, and as he walked and turned the noises got nearer. Jollity flew on ahead as far as he could and as high as he could; he could make out the pattern of the maze in the murk. He flew back and settled on Tom's shoulder. 'I hope you are doing the right thing.'

'I hope I am too, Jollity,' Tom said.

Some flickers of light glimmered ahead, and when Tom turned the next corner he could see shadows moving on the walls. Shadows he recognized well enough.

He had nearly reached the centre of the maze, it seemed. The smell was worse here. He could dimly see his father standing in front of a group of figures. The princesses were no longer chained together and he could make out Rapunzel by her hair. She was working on the chains that linked his brothers, as were other shadowy figures, while his father stood tall with his arms wide as if he were protecting them all, but from what?

Tom soon found out.

As Tom turned the final corner of the maze he saw, towering over Big Jack, a huge man. He was broad shouldered and had a thickly muscled body bursting out of ragged clothes. Tom could see that he also had a tail which dragged on the floor behind him. In one hand the creature held a flaming torch, which showed the huge head of a bull, with long curving horns and a mane of thick matted bull hair all down his wide neck.

'I should put your wolf pelt cloak on, Tom,' Jollity said, 'it worked before.'

Tom crouched down and rummaged in his bag. He pulled out the Norse cloak and wrapped it round his shoulders. At the same time he unrolled the length of shimmering gold cloth that he had stuffed in there after he had escaped from the palace with Ariadne; he thought that it might be useful too. He draped it round his middle and tucked the ends of it into his belt. Then he walked into the arena sized space keeping his back to the wall. His sword glowed a kind of dulled blood red.

Big Jack saw him first, and put a chained hand up as if telling Tom to keep away. The bull-headed creature, the Minotaur, turned and saw Tom too. It roared and Tom could clearly see lumps and gobbets of mucus flying out from its horrible mouth. Its eyes glowed and widened at the sight of Tom, a fresh victim. It stamped forward a pace and Tom could see in the dim torch-light that it wore a few vestiges of rusty bloodied armour, a torn tunic, and a pair of ruined sandal boots tied on to its feet. It raised its huge arms, opened its mouth and roared again so that the walls of the labyrinth seemed to wobble and bits of stone shifted and fell.

'No, Tom, go,' Big Jack shouted.

Rapunzel stood up and pointed to Tom and all his brothers called out to him as well.

'Go away, Tom, now, save yourself,' they cried, 'run!'

Tom didn't run away. He felt confident that Hafnir's wolf cloak would protect him with the spirit of Fenrir the giant wolf, just as it had done when he had been attacked by those brigands on the road.

He walked forward further into the big space, into the dark heart of the Labyrinth. The smell was worse than ever here, and Tom caught terrible glimpses out of the corner of his eye, of what looked like rotting carcasses, rib cages, and human skulls all piled up in a mound at the back. He couldn't let this happen to them, his family were not meat, were not a sacrifice. He marched into the very centre of the arena. Jollity flew beside him and settled on his shoulder.

'That is the worst thing yet,' he said nervously in Tom's ear.

The Minotaur turned to face Tom directly. It lowered its huge head between its shoulders, and snorted and pawed the ground with one foot.

'It's getting ready to charge, Tom,' Jollity said.

'I can see it, old friend. You fly off, go on now.'

The crow lifted from Tom's shoulder and flew across the space between Tom and the Minotaur. The Minotaur lifted its head and then swiped out at the crow with the flaming torch in its hand. The flames missed Jollity but the shadow of the bird loomed large suddenly on the back wall.

'Throw me the sword, Tom,' Big Jack shouted, 'and then run.'

At once Tom threw the sword and Big Jack caught it by the handle. In the hand of its maker the sword burst into light. A great shower of golden sparks and blinding beams shot out from it, lighting up the whole arena for a split second. Tom could see everything: his brothers and their wives cowering against the back wall, and Big Jack suddenly slicing through his own chains. The Minotaur was both lit up and dazzled by the burst of bright light. It looked, if anything, pitiful, ugly and tragic. It charged past Tom, stumbled, and turned again in a fury. It flung the flaming torch at him. Tom wasted no time. He dodged the flames and then turned and ran away back out into the maze corridor and the Minotaur followed him.

Tom could hear heavy breathing and stamping feet behind him. Tom hoped that Jollity was somewhere near, flying in the darkness. Tom saw his own shadow suddenly leap forward along the dark beaten earth in front of him. The shadow was caused by the bright light from his birthday sword. Big Jack had followed them out into the narrow passageway. He heard the Minotaur roar and bellow. Tom squeezed himself close against the smooth wall and turned.

Big Jack had stamped on the Minotaur's tail, and stood blocking the way back holding the sword in both hands. The Minotaur turned and roared, Big Jack lunged forward with the sword, and the Minotaur lowered its bull head and charged. Each dashed past the other. The sword struck the smooth wall in a shower of blazing golden sparks. The Minotaur hit the opposite wall, bellowed and turned again, tugging at its tail. Jollity appeared and flew straight at the bull's head. The creature tried to bat Jollity away, but the bird was too quick for it and veered upwards, allowing Big Jack to get a sword blow across its back.

The Minotaur howled and spun round and charged at Jack, who dodged aside so that the Minotaur struck the wall. Tom clearly saw part of one of its horns break off. The beast howled and roared again, and raised its hands to feel the damaged horn in surprise. Big Jack side-stepped and gestured for Tom to fall back. The Minotaur lowered its head once more and Tom could see steam rising from its nostrils. Then it charged Big Jack, and finally connected with him, the flat of its head turning Jack aside and tossing him into the air. The Minotaur roared.

'Dad!' Tom called out.

'It's all right,' Big Jack called out.

Tom looked behind the Minotaur and saw his brothers all still chained together blocking the entrance back to the arena. The Minotaur charged them down and they fell back in a heap and one of the princesses screamed.

Big Jack struggled up from the ground, pulling himself up with the sword. Tom could see that he was weakened and shaking. Jollity swooped down again and flew all around the Minotaur's head, flapping his black wings, being as confusing as he could be. This time the Minotaur easily batted him away. Tom took his bow from his shoulder, loaded an arrow and fired directly at the monster. The arrow caught in its chest and hung there. Tom fired another and missed, and then another, and again the arrow caught in the monster's chest and Tom could see blood.

'Go on, Tom,' he heard shouted out from among his chained brothers. Before he could reach for another arrow, Big Jack was striding forward, with the bright flashing sword held out in front of him. Tom pulled the shining gold cloth out from his belt and held it out wide in his hands. The light from the sword reflected back from the gold cloth and dazzled the Minotaur, and it raised its arms over its eyes. Jack leaped forward and it seemed then as if the Minoataur and Big Jack were dancing together among the shadows and flashes of reflected gold light. Tom dropped the cloth and the dark returned and so he could not see clearly enough between the two struggling figures to fire his last remaining arrow.

The two figures thrashed and bounced between the

narrow walls, the Minotaur snorting and howling in rage. Tom could just make out Big Jack held close in the monster's arms. It seemed as if it were crushing him.

The birthday sword fell to the ground and its glow darkened and then went out. And then Big Jack was dropped and slumped down beside it. The Minotaur let out a huge roar of triumph. It turned its back on Tom and roared once again at the line of sprawled and chained brothers. Big Jack lay perfectly still on the ground.

Tom stood looking in disbelief at the broad and bloodied back of the terrible beast. He felt a strong twitch on the gold thread looped loosely in his hand. It was as if Ariadne, all the way up above near the gate, in the bright light of day, was sending him a message of encouragement. Tom felt a sudden surge of furious energy, and an almost blinding rush of anger. He ran forward and picked up his birthday sword on the run. He jumped up in the air as high as he could, and as he jumped the sword brightened again in his hand and he slashed wildly at the Minotaur.

Tom fell back on to the earth still holding his sword.

He lay on his back with his eyes closed, waiting for the blow from the Minotaur. It didn't come.

He heard a voice in his ear. 'Tom, are you all right?' It was Jollity, and Tom opened his eyes. Lying on the ground between him and Big Jack was the bull's head of the Minotaur. It had been cleanly sliced from its body in one hit. Tom scrambled to his feet and lurched over to his father.

Big Jack lay completely still on the ground. Tom pressed his ear to his father's chest but could hear nothing. It seemed that the Minotaur had crushed him to death.

Tom stayed very still. As still as the body of his father, his kindly brave father. Tom kept his head pressed close to his father's chest: it was still warm. He put his arm out and round his father's body and pressed himself as hard as he could against Big Jack. 'Dad,' he said quietly.

'He died defending his family, Tom,' said Jollity quietly. 'He died as an adventurer and a brave man.'

'What is it, Tom, what's happened?' Jacques asked from the huddle of chained brothers.

One of the princesses stepped forward from the

arena beyond the line of brothers. She knelt and put her arms around Tom.

'Ariadne told me that in here was the worst thing in the world,' said Tom quietly, 'and she was right.'

'Can't be true, no, not Big Jack,' said Jackie.

'Our father, no, no, I don't believe it,' said Jackson. 'Not after all that.'

'I will kill Ormestone myself, with my bare hands,' said Jacques, before bursting into tears.

Jollity said quietly, 'Tom.'

'What is it, Jollity?' Tom said without looking up at his old friend.

'Do you remember what happened just before you defeated the Cyclops?'

'The Cyclops?' Tom mumbled.

'Monster with one eye. There was an old man, an oracle. Remember now, Tom, the water from the sacred spring, remember what he said?'

Tom suddenly let go of his father, sat up and threw off his travel bag. He knelt down and rummaged through it by the flickering light of his birthday sword. 'I do remember,' he said excitedly, pulling out the stone ginger beer bottle from the muddle inside.

'Nice thought, Tom, at a time like this,' said Jackson quietly. 'A little of our mother's ginger beer, a taste of home, eh?'

'Home,' whispered Jake, 'home.'

'Just wait,' said Tom, and he opened the stone bottle and then turned and lifted Big Jack's head and rested it on the bunched up length of gold cloth. He put the neck of the bottle against Big Jack's mouth, forcing it gently between his lips. He tipped some of the water from the bottle into his father's mouth. He tipped it twice more, trickling a little more of the water each time.

Tom stoppered the bottle, sat back on his haunches and waited. All his chained brothers were by now on their knees, and their princess brides had their heads bowed. There was a long moment of silence.

Tom studied his father's kindly face for any sign of movement.

Tom's birthday sword suddenly glowed a little brighter, and the gold cloth under Big Jack's head reflected the sudden change in light. There was a cough, and Tom suddenly shot upright on to his feet. His father coughed again and the sword glowed brighter still.

'What was that, Tom?' Jacques called out.

Before Tom could answer Big Jack sat up and rubbed his head. 'What's happened, Tom?' he said.

'Tom slew the Minotaur,' said Jollity. 'Took its head off in one vengeful blow; it wouldn't have felt a thing. It knocked you out, sir, but luckily Tom has just revived you.'

Big Jack stood up and stretched his arms wide.

'Well, I'll be, who would have thought our mother's ginger beer was that powerful,' said Jackie with a chuckle. The other brothers all laughed with him in relief.

'Not a word, Tom,' said Jollity, 'you hero.'

'We must get out of here,' said Big Jack. 'An impossible task in this huge awful maze, we will all most likely starve.'

'No need to starve,' said Tom. 'I tied the end of this gold thread to one of the entrance doors. We just need to follow it back.'

Tom gave a strong tug on the thread to let Ariadne know that he was safe.

Big Jack picked up the hideous head of the Minotaur and wrapped it up in the gold cloth and tied the ends. 'I shall look forward to giving this to Ormestone as a gift,' he said, and hefted it on to his back.

'Lead the way then, our Tom,' he said. 'Ready?'

'I'm ready,' said Tom.

'We're all ready,' came the chorus of chained brothers and their princess wives.

'After you, Tom,' said Big Jack, 'after you.' They all began the long climb back to the light of day.

Chapter 36

ON THE BEACH

10.38 P.M.

Tom led them all the way back up through the dark passageways to the entrance chamber. Ariadne was there patiently waiting. She ran forward and flung her arms around Tom.

'You are safe, you are all safe,' she said.

'Thanks to Tom and your clever thinking,' said Big Jack. 'I am Jack, Tom's father. Thank you for your help. These chained-up boys are my other sons, Jake, Jackson, Jackie, Jacques, Jack, and Jacquot, and their brides are with them too. Introduce yourselves, girls,' he added, 'I have never met you properly before myself after all.'

327

One by one the princesses nodded their heads and introduced themselves.

'I am sorry, Ariadne,' said Big Jack, 'but your nice gold cloth has been ruined, I am afraid.' And he held the bloodstained gold bundle up high.

Ariadne shrank back at the sight of it. 'Tom destroyed the monster,' said Big Jack, 'and its head is in here.'

Tom looked down and shook his head. 'It looked sad and scared,' said Tom, 'I almost feel sorry for it.'

'It killed and ate dozens of our innocent young people, Tom,' said Ariadne, 'young people just like us, Tom, and your brothers. You did the right thing.'

'Ariadne's right, Tom,' said Jollity.

'Three cheers for our Tom,' said Jack the younger.

'No time for that, I'm afraid,' Big Jack said quickly, 'later. We have to leave now and work out a way to get back to the city and finish Ormestone for good. Then we can celebrate.'

Big Jack led the way out on to the black beach. It was dark and there were stars out. There was a line of lit flaming torches blazing all the way down to the shoreline. A group of shadowy figures stood on the beach near the doors to the Labyrinth. One of them stepped forward balancing on a crutch.

'Arrrgh,' he said, 'if it ain't young Tom Trueheart I see there.' It was the peg-legged pirate from the Admiral Benbowe inn. A great shout went up from the brothers and their brides.

'Have no fear, ladies and gents, we 'ave no quarrel with you. We want only one thing: the gold that's owing to us.'

Big Jack stepped forward to meet the pirate captain halfway.

'There is gold enough here for any ransom; a king's treasure, I am told, in the chamber here.'

'Arrrgh, there's the thing; 'tis guarded by a monstrous something, see,' said the pirate. 'How to get at it?'

'Guarded by two monstrous things,' said Big Jack, 'both gone, both dead.'

''Ow do we know that,' said the pirate. 'Where's yer proof, see.'

'Look around you,' said Jack, and he took one of the flaming torches out of the sand and walked over to the monstrous golden head lying half buried on the beach. 'All that remains of the giant Talos, guardian of the old king's treasure.'

'Aaargh, yer said there was another monster,' said the pirate captain.

'Yes,' said Big Jack, 'the Minotaur, a fearful thing, half man half bull.' He walked back to the huddle of Truehearts and pulled out the gold bundle. He crouched down, and plunged the torch into the sand, then he unwrapped the gold cloth and revealed the ragged severed bull's head.

The pirates came near as a group, took one look at the mess on the sand and then quickly stepped back again, with grumbles of disgust.

'The treasure's yours for the taking,' Big Jack said. 'Help yourselves.'

'Pieces of eight, pieces of eight,' said the parrot perched on the captain's shoulder, excitedly.

'Arrgh, we will, my friend, we will,' said the pirate grinning from ear to earringed ear. 'Come on, lads, for'ard and fill yer boots.'

The pirates moved towards the doors carrying sacks and lugging treasure chests between them.

'There's more, though,' said Big Jack, 'much more.'

'More, yer say?' said the captain. 'Where might that be?'

'I'll tell you,' said Big Jack, 'but we would need a favour from you in return.'

Chapter 37

THE GOLD IN THE CITY

Ormestone had Rumpelstiltskin taken back to his villa under heavy escort. The city was still festive enough with all the gold banners and flags, but the streets themselves were deserted. It was as if no one wanted to celebrate with the terrible events going on in the labyrinth over the water, even though the city's own young had been spared.

The low sun streamed in through the wide doorway with the view of the sea and the dark island. Ormestone dismissed the guards from the room. It was looking especially splendid with all the gold piled upon gold; the dragon's hoard and the rest of it, all lit up and made even more golden by the setting sun.

'Look at it, gold, lovely sprite gold,' said Ormestone, raising his gold-sleeved arms wide and gesturing around at the whole scene.

Rumpelstiltskin stared at the floor.

'Over there the final unhappy end of the Truehearts and their miserable tales. Here a ray of golden light falls upon all my gold and soon it will be your chance,' he said pointing at Rumpelstiltskin, 'to finally and fully redeem yourself.'

'Redeem myself, majesty,' Rumpelstiltskin mumbled, 'how?'

'Surely you haven't fogotten our conversation, our recent conversation?'

'I think I remember it.'

'I should hope so too. Grant me that one thing tomorrow and you will be freed, your wand will be returned, and all shall be well with you. Guards,' he called out, 'take him and lock him up. Bring him back at dawn, the golden hour. I must rest and be ready for my final act of greatness.'

Rumpelstiltskin was led away to the room in the cellar where Big Jack Trueheart had once been locked. He sat slumped and unhappy on the floor, his back against the wall, with only the faint starlight at the window for company.

My princesses are lost, he thought, and sighed to himself. At least I freed them from their bonds at the last, and tomorrow I shall carry out one last act, one more request, and he allowed himself a brief smile.

The pirates, loaded down with the king's gold from the dark island, set sail for the city harbour. The Truehearts and their brides all sat together happily on the deck. They had enjoyed a feast with the pirates and the ship's smith had freed the brothers from their sprite chains with brute force and cunning.

The peg-legged captain was in a good mood, too. He had a mound of treasure in his bilges as was his right as an honourable pirate, and he was also about to make good a terrible wrong. A wrong carried out under duress and without honour. Honour would be restored to the pirates, a rare thing indeed.

Tom, Jollity, and Ariadne sat slightly apart from the others. Tom was looking up at the night sky.

'I feel bad about what I had to do, Jollity. I killed a creature, I ended a life with my own hands.'

'That's true, Tom,' said Jollity, 'but it was going to kill you, and your father, and all your brothers and their wives too, and eventually even young Ariadne here. You acted as you did and bravely for the greater good, you had no choice.'

'I wasn't really brave,' said Tom, 'just blinded by fury. I wonder if the spirit of the Minotaur is up there now in the sky.' He pointed up. 'Those stars there look a bit like a bull.'

'More likely that you will be up there in the sky one day, Tom, the constellation of an archer with his bow, or a swordsman with his sword,' said Ariadne.

Further down the deck in the captain's cabin, Big Jack and the captain laid their plans for the morning.

'We are agreed then?' said Big Jack. 'You may have

the king's gold, and anything we may find apart from the dragon's hoard, which Tom has promised to return.'

'Arrrgh, aye, right enough,' said the captain, 'agreed,' and they shook hands.

'Pieces of eight,' said the parrot.

'To the morning, then,' said the captain raising his tankard of rum.

'To the morning,' said Big Jack, raising his own cup.

The next morning dawned a flawless bright gold over the horizon. Ormestone was awake and on his terrace overlooking the sea. Although it was early he had still missed the shadowy arrival of the disguised pirate ship into the harbour in the early hours. Since then the wind had dropped, and all the golden banners across the city hung limply from the flagpoles. He finished his breakfast: some gilded grapes, a golden apple, and some breakfast wine made from honey. He summoned the guards to bring Rumpelstiltskin to him. The scruffy little sprite was soon standing sweltering in the heat of the morning.

'A beautiful morning, don't you think?'

'Oh yes, your majesty,' said Rumpelstiltskin uncomfortably, mournfully.

'You don't sound very happy on this most perfect day of days,' said Ormestone.

'Well, sire, I have lost my loves, my princesses,' he said.

'There will be other princesses for you, all over the Land of Stories. Why, I seem to remember in a planning meeting someone once came up with the idea of twelve dancing princesses as a concept,' Ormestone replied, the sun casting shadows across his face.

'Would that be a promise, majesty?'

'More of a hope than a promise, but if the story has been developed then there they will be, all twelve of them to choose from.'

'We are no longer in the Land of Stories though, majesty.'

'True, very true,' said Ormestone, 'but to that end I had the captain of the guard send the stitched-faced fellow and that Cyclops off to repair my flying machine and get it ready to make your way back there.'

'Will you not return with us, majesty?' said Rumpelstiltskin, keeping his gaze lowered and his voice mournful.

'I know that I belong here, and with the cowed and grateful populace and the power you are about to grant me I can achieve anything. I can build the biggest and best-paid army the world has ever seen. I can influence the outcome of all future stories for ever just as I vowed the day we landed here. I can lay the building blocks for the future and then when I am ready, I will travel forward and outwards across the boundary sea and there my world will be waiting just as I should like it. Enough of that for now. Time, I think.'

'Time, majesty?' said Rumpelstiltskin.

'Time to grant my greatest wish.'

'Oh yes, that. I will need my wand back, your majesty.'

Ormestone called a guard forward who produced the shabby little stick on a velvet cushion. Ormestone took it and held it out to Rumpelstiltskin.

'You promise me that this will really work?'

'I am sure of it, majesty,' Rumpelstiltskin said. He reached his short arm out and took the little wand. At last, Rumpelstiltskin thought. Now it must be done. My princesses are gone for ever, and in a foul way too, all much too horrible to think about. Finally Ormestone must really pay.

Ormestone spread his arms out wide and turned his face to the golden sunlight which streamed now across the terrace. 'The moment is here, the time is right, I am ready, my lovelorn little friend.'

The word 'lovelorn' burned itself hard into Rumpelstiltskin, and he simmered with a terrible fury while trying to keep himself outwardly calm. The moment had finally arrived. He pointed his wand across at his gold-robed master and opened his mouth.

The Truehearts, Ariadne, and the gang of fully armed pirates made their way through the dawn streets of the city, while Jollity flew on ahead. He found the palace and flew in through an open window, and following directions from Ariadne he flew down the long corridors to the golden throne room. It was empty, there was no sign of any guards or of Ormestone himself. He left and flew on further to the king's villa and there he saw him: Ormestone, standing on his terrace in the growing dawn light. He circled a few times to make sure and then flew back to where Tom and the others were waiting.

'He is at his villa not at the palace,' Jollity said to Tom, and flew off again, back to the villa and settled on the roof above the terrace. He quietly folded his wings and waited.

The little rag-tag army came stealthily up the hill to the villa. The single guard at the gate was soon over-powered. Tom drew his sword ready and they all went into the villa itself.

It was difficult for the pirate captain not to cry out in joy at the sight of all the gold piled up everywhere as they walked past all the gold-filled rooms and barred chambers. At the end of the corridor they could see the bright light of the open terrace.

Jollity had seen them all coming from his position up on the red-tiled roof. He flew down and landed very lightly on the balustrade of Ormestone's terrace but a few inches from Ormestone himself. Rumpelstiltskin saw Jollity at once but made no sign of recognition. His wand was poised in his hand and pointing at

Ormestone and he was about to speak; nothing would deflect him.

'I grant you, Julius Ormestone, story deviser, a sprite sacred power, to wit, that everything you touch will turn at once into pure sprite gold.' A little crackle and spark passed from the wand to Ormestone himself.

'That is not exactly what we agreed,' said Ormestone, a surge of strange energy coursing suddenly through him.

Tom was the first of them out on to the bright terrace. He ran across the short space towards Ormestone with his birthday sword raised. Ormestone took in at once what was happening and smiled a terrible smile. He extended his hands towards Tom who was hurtling at him across the terrace. At that moment his hands touched something black which had flown up suddenly and got in his way. That same something fell with a heavy thump. Tom stopped in shock at what had just happened, and looked down at the thing which lay at Ormestone's feet. It was Jollity the crow, only now he was made of pure solid sprite gold.

Ormestone looked up at Tom and his smile broadened even further. Behind them the doorway to the terrace was suddenly crowded with a confusion of pirates, Truehearts, and princesses.

Rumpelstiltskin saw his girls free and unharmed and his heart lifted.

Tom screamed in anger, 'Jollity!' and then he lunged forward the last few inches towards Ormestone's outstretched hands.

'Majesty,' Rumpelstiltskin screamed out, 'your face!'

Ormestone raised his hands to his own face automatically. In an instant, and in a blaze of golden sunlight he turned into a solid sprite gold statue of himself, his hands raised and a curious and ridiculous expression on his face.

Tom bumped into the solid gold thing and fell over. He sat for a moment looking at the statue's seven-league booted gold feet. He stood then and struck at it with his sword; some sparks flickered from the edge of the blade. Tom put down his sword and picked up the gold bird instead.

'The crow sacrificed himself for you, Tom Trueheart,' Rumpelstiltskin said.

'Rumply,' said Princess Zinnia, 'what have you done?'

'I simply granted my foolish master's greatest wish, my beauty,' he replied, and he turned the wand and pointed it instead at the golden bird.

'What are you doing?' Jackson called out, but Rumpelstiltskin took no notice. He muttered something and the golden bird darkened at once. It turned black suddenly in Tom's arms and then flew upwards in a shower of bright sunlit sparks.

'Jollity,' Tom called out in delight.

'Hello, Tom,' he called back.

Princess Sleeping Beauty stepped forward from the doorway and put her arms around Rumpelstiltskin and kissed him on both cheeks. 'Well done, Rumply,' she said, 'you did the right thing at last.' Then all the princesses and Jill ran over and hugged and kissed him.

'Steady on, Jill,' Little Jack said. 'We have come to finish that fiend off once and for all as well as Ormestone.'

Big Jack stepped in. 'Tom told me that he thought you had helped him earlier, and it seems he was right.' He went over to the golden statue of Ormestone and tapped on it. 'Solid?' he said to Rumpelstiltskin.

'Oh yes, solid, and permanent. I have no wish to bring him back, ever.'

'We would all agree with that,' Big Jack said. 'I don't know what we should do with you, Rumpelstiltskin. We will decide on our journey back.'

One by one all the Trueheart brothers came over and tapped or kicked at the golden statue just to make sure of it.

The pirate captain said, 'Aargh, 'tis a valuable thing that statue, being more or less made of solid sprite doubloons.'

'Pieces of eight,' said his parrot.

'Pieces of more than just eight, my fine bird.' The captain walked round the statue.

'I promised Tabitha the Cat a good reward for bringing me over here and for waiting to take me back,' said Tom. 'I should give some to her by rights.'

'We'll cut it up,' said Big Jack. 'Some to our pirate friends, some to your Cat girl, Tom. Would she have room for me on her boat as well, do you think?'

'I am sure she would, but it's a small boat; what about everybody else?'

'I rather thought these rascally pirates might take them back to the Isle of Happy Ever After, seeing that they brought them from there in the first place under duress.'

'Why, aaarrgh, t'would be a proper honour,' said the pirate captain saluting Big Jack and causing his parrot to fly up in surprise.

The city elders were summoned to a meeting at the palace. Big Jack took to the podium.

'Your recent king was in fact an evil man. He had all of you under some sort of spell. He was after only two things: the power to control stories for ever and gold. He wanted to alter the nature of stories and bend them all to his twisted vision. And he wanted the gold both to glorify himself and to pay for his terrible schemes. You should elect a new king, a new city leader, a fair-minded person, who can rule this fine city without fear.'

One of the elders, Daedalus, stepped forward. 'We cannot live without fear, what of the beast that I helped imprison on the dark island and his demands?'

'That monster is dead,' Jack said. 'Killed with one blow by my son Tom here.'

'With respect,' said Daedalus, 'he is only a young boy. How do we know that this is true?'

'Here is the proof, all the way from those stinking tunnels of yours,' said Big Jack, and he unrolled the length of bloodied gold fabric to reveal the monstrous rotting head of the Minotaur. A cry of shock and horror went up in the hall.

'As you see, it can trouble you no further, your children are safe; the curse is lifted,' said Big Jack. 'Nor will that rotten king trouble you, except perhaps in your dreams and stories. The monstrous half man, half bull in his labyrinth, and the greedy king who turned himself into gold: some good stories to tell your children there and no mistake.'

Chapter 38

The gold statue of Ormestone was so heavy it had to be taken down to the harbour on rollers. The pirates processed it through the quiet streets pushing barrowfuls and trunkloads of gold alongside it. The flags were blowing in the fresh breeze as if the end of Ormestone had lifted a heavy spell from the weather as well. Tom was glad to see the dragon's hoard being carried safely on board in a separate chest.

'Wait,' he said, and he reached into his travel bag and pulled out all the coins that Big Jack had left on the road as clues.

'Mustn't miss any of it out, that clever dragon will know,' he said.

Ariadne was standing at the bottom of the gangplank.

'It was nice meeting you, and helping you, and knowing you, Tom Trueheart,' she said, 'and you too, Jollity. I still think it's a funny sort of name, though, Tom Trueheart,' and she giggled, just as she had when they first met. Then she leaned forward and kissed Tom once on the cheek.

Tom blushed.

'I shall tell my own children the story of the Minotaur one day,' she said, 'but I might choose another name for the hero, one of our native names instead. Would you mind if I did that?'

'Of course I wouldn't,' Tom said, 'all stories change with the teller and the telling. We adventurers and storytellers know that, we expect it. Well, goodbye then, Ariadne.' And he walked up the gangplank with Jollity bobbing on his shoulder, turned once and waved back to her.

Ariadne, Daedalus, and a small solemn handful of city elders stood on the quayside and waved the ship away as it left the harbour.

Tom pointed out the place on the chart; the rock formation where he was due to meet Tabitha and the pea-green boat. Before that, of course, he would have to return the dragon's hoard, and for that he would need to find Hafnir and Sigurd and their good ship *Dragon Helm Twenty Oars*.

The pirate ship sailed on through the warm starry night and Tom and his father stayed up on deck. Jollity settled down to sleep with his head tucked under his wing.

Big Jack pointed to the horizon. 'At some point soon we will come to the boundary sea. I have crossed it before. We have to hope we come out in our own time, or as close to when you left as we can get,' Big Jack said.

'I need to look out for the warriors' ship that saved me from the Kraken,' said Tom.

'We shall do that, my boy, don't worry.' And Big Jack put his arm round Tom's shoulder and gave him a squeeze. 'It will be good to be back, but strange too.

I haven't seen your mother in a long while, not since you were a baby.'

'I know,' said Tom sleepily.

'You sleep, Tom, rest your head. I'll wake you at any sign of a warrior ship.'

Tom nestled against his father's shoulder and slipped into a dreamless sleep.

His father gently shook him awake. Tom stirred and sat up. Jollity was awake too and the pirate ship was now surrounded by a thick sea mist. Lights and colours glowed through the fog as if lanterns were passing by them at speed.

'The boundary sea, Tom,' said Big Jack.

The peg-legged captain was soon beside them on deck.

'This must be where we was taken off course 'afore,' he said. 'But comin' the other way, aarrgh. I remember this, it was like nothin' none of us 'ad seen 'afore.'

The ship sailed on through the mist and gradually all Tom's brothers and their wives came up on deck too.

There was a sudden call from the lookout on the mainmast. 'Ship ahoy.'

'Battle stations, lads,' the peg-legged captain cried at once. 'It'll be the excise men.'

Tom asked for the captain's spyglass. He looked across through the thinning mist. 'Don't worry, captain,' he said. 'It's not the excise men, it's the ship I was hoping to find. This is where we must leave you.'

The two ships hove to broadside on. On one side were the pirates and the Truehearts, with their rows of cannon, and on the other were Hafnir and Sigurd and their oarsmen and their line of bright copper shields.

Tom waved across at Hafnir, and Hafnir, standing proud in his horned helmet, waved back.

The big statue of Ormestone was hauled up from the bilges along with little Rumpelstiltskin. The ship's smithy attacked the statue with a saw. Rumpelstiltskin watched as his old master lost his head for the last time.

'Pieces of eight,' the parrot cried as the golden head was neatly sliced off from the shoulders.

'I was brought to these waters originally by a very

brave girl in a pea-green boat,' said Tom. 'And you remember I said I had promised her a fine gold reward for her trouble.'

'Course,' said the pirate captain.

'Do you think you could saw off a good lump for her now as well while you are at it?'

'Course we can, plenty here to go round.'

The body was sawn through again at the waist.

'You can keep the feet and legs, captain, then,' said Tom. He wrapped the heavy golden head up in his packstaff bundle. The other lump of gold was lowered in a bundle down to the pirate's rowing boat.

Big Jack stepped forward. 'What to do with our little friend Rumpelstiltskin here?' he said.

'Arrrgh,' said the peg-legged captain, 'smithy can cut his head off too if you like, aarrgh.'

'Good idea,' said Jacques, and the other brothers laughed.

'No,' said Snow White, 'don't do that. Poor old Rumply, he did save Tom and Tom saved all of us, so in a way Rumply saved us too.'

'Quite right,' said Zinnia.

'Here here,' said Cinderella.

'I have an idea,' said Rapunzel.

'Are you thinking what I am thinking?' said Jill.

'He can work for us,' said Rapunzel, 'take it in turns, a few weeks with each of us. Little bits of sprite magic here and there, a little fetching and carrying. You never know, there might be the blessing of babies soon. We would need protection from spells and changelings and bad faeries of all sorts.'

Rumpelstiltskin beamed with delight at this idea; hope sprang up in his little heart: his lovely princesses to care for, could it really happen?

The brothers went into a huddle.

Tom said, 'He did save me, he opened my cell door.'

'All right,' Jackie said.

'But the girls will look after his wand,' Jackson added. 'No magic at all except under their rules and supervision.'

'Agreed,' said Rumpelstiltskin, 'magic tires me out at the best of times.' He was already dreaming of the nice cold forests of home and a new life of happiness and service to come.

'All agreed then?' said Jake.

'Agreed,' the brothers chorused.

Tom, Big Jack, and Jollity bade farewell to Jacques, Jackie, Jackson, Jake, Jack, and Jacquot, and Zinnia, Jill, Sleeping Beauty, Cinderella, Rapunzel, and Snow White, and the peg-legged captain and his parrot and all his rascally crew.

They were rowed across the short stretch of boundary sea to the waiting Norse ship. As Tom clambered on board he remembered to take the wolf pelt cloak out of his travel bag.

Chapter 39

' . . . And then I opened the chest right in front of her and there was all the dragon's hoard, every last coin. The dragon was very pleased and Uhn celebrated by making us some bacon and eggs on an outside fire, which the dragon very kindly lit for us before she set off back to her cave in the mountain with her hoard. And as we ate the delicious breakfast the sky lightened up, the clouds seemed to dissolve away and the breeze felt all warm suddenly. There was a spread of colour too across the mountain as all the bright spring flowers opened up everywhere, one after the other.

' "The winter has passed," Uhn said, "no more Fimbul, no Ragnarok for now," and he smiled.

'Then Hafnir took us out to the rocks where Tabitha and her pea-green boat were waiting for us, and I gave her the great lump of sprite gold which would at least pay for a smart new dinghy, the Kraken having sunk the other one. And then we came straight here from the harbour to tell our story to you all.' Tom looked over at Big Jack who smiled and nodded back at him.

There was applause. The Master called for silence by raising his arms, and eventually the hall went quiet.

'I would like to thank Tom Trueheart,' said the Master, 'most warmly for completing, and then sharing with us, his big adventure. The whole of the Trueheart family has shown, as usual, exceptional courage . . . '

Tom held up his arm and interrupted the master. 'I almost forgot, one more thing, Master,' he said. He took his packstaff and unwrapped the heart cloth and lifted something out and put it on to the lectern. A gasp went round the hall, for there sat the neatly severed golden head of Bro. J. Ormestone, story deviser second class.

'A first exhibit for the museum of stories,' Tom said. There was another thunderous round of applause.

'Best kept strictly under lock and key,' said the Master, edging away from the golden head with its strange pair of hands attached to the face. He carried on with his speech.

'Tom has done more than thoroughly live up to the noble name of Trueheart, but then we would hardly expect any less from a member of the last of the great adventuring families.' More loud applause followed this too.

'To have brought back your dear father, Jack the Giant Killer, when he was lost to us for so long and to have thoroughly defeated the wicked Ormestone too, the terrible evidence of which we now have before us, deserves our highest praise and gratitude. Our new stories will certainly flourish now. Why, as it happens, just today I ordered that twelve dancing princesses were to be got ready to practise for their own new adventure.'

More applause followed on, and Tom had a sudden thought about Rumpelstiltskin somewhere off on the Isle of Happy Ever After protecting his princesses. Someone had mentioned there might soon be babies to protect too, and so some time in the future perhaps, Tom thought, I might not be the last of the Truehearts after all?

When Tom and his father finally left the Story Bureau it was late in the afternoon. There was a chill in the air and Tom could almost smell the snow that would surely fall soon. Because of crossing the boundary sea they had arrived back in the Land of Stories in the late autumn and it was now very close to Tom's thirteenth birthday. Jollity rode on Tom's shoulder as they made their way back through the quiet woods towards Tom's little house.

Big Jack saw the house suddenly, nestled as ever among the trees at the edge of the forest, close to the crossroads that led to Four Gates Road. The house was in darkness and would appear to be fast asleep, except for the thin ribbon of smoke that drifted from the chimney, and the faint light of a night lantern, which hung from the eaves of the little porch and seemed to say 'welcome, traveller'. He stopped on the path just out of view of the windows.

'I'm nervous, Tom, I've been a long time away. It's given me a funny turn; my tummy rolled over then, from just seeing the old place again . . . '

'It'll be all right, Dad,' said Tom. 'Come on, not much further now.'

Mrs Trueheart was about to lock up the house as she did every night while everyone was away. She had a feeling that it might snow that night and she opened the front door to look out at the sky. The white clouds were massing above the trees but some of the stars were still clear. Something made her walk out from the porch a little way. A movement caught her eye near the far treeline.

'Is that you, Tom?' she called out.

She could see two figures now, both with pack-staffs over their shoulders. One very much taller than the other.

'Tom?' she said.

The taller figure moved slowly into the light from the porch lantern and took his packstaff down from his shoulder.

Tom and Jollity watched from the treeline. The two figures, his mother and his long-lost father, suddenly ran into each other's arms. Tom watched his father hugging his mother for sheer joy. It was the first time he had seen this happen in his whole life.

'Little walk now, Tom, in the woods; I have an appointment there soon,' Jollity said, after what seemed a long moment.

Tom stayed still for a minute longer watching his mother and father, happy that he had done everything that he had promised. Then he said, 'Come on then, Jollity, best leave them alone for a while.'

They walked through the cold woods together.

'Wait here a moment, Tom,' Jollity said, and flew off suddenly and settled on a branch of the special old oak tree. An owl hooted, tree branches creaked. Then Tom heard the light crackle of a sprite footfall across the fallen leaves. It was old Cicero Brownfield himself coming down the path towards them. The sprite tipped his head in a nod to Tom.

'Heard you brought Big Jack back with you, Tom,' he said, 'well done.'

Cicero walked over to the old oak and looked up at Jollity. Then Cicero said something very quietly which Tom couldn't catch. The crow seemed to shiver suddenly on the branch. There was a brief dazzle of bright star shapes as a transformation took place in front of an astonished Tom.

A sprite suddenly stepped out of the tree shadow. He shook his shoulders and stretched out his arms and fingers.

'Well well,' said Cicero, 'so there you are, young Jollity. No longer I think an apprentice sprite, after what you two have achieved.'

'Thank you, Cicero,' said Jollity, and then he looked over at Tom.

'Hello, Tom,' he said, 'first time you've seen me as myself.'

'Yes,' said Tom. In front of him was a sprite of about his own age and height, dressed in mossy greens and earth colours, and complete with a little circlet of leaves in his wild hair. They looked into each other's eyes for a brief moment. Tom reached his hand out and Jollity took it in his.

'Friends?' said Jollity.

'Always,' said Tom.

Cicero said, 'I think we can all congratulate ourselves on jobs well done. Excellent work indeed, especially from you, Tom. The golden head of Ormestone, my, my,' and he clapped Tom on the back. 'Come on, we should away, we will most likely have some new story letters to deliver soon, and there will be many new adventures to arrange, and I should think some of those letters might well be for you, Tom Trueheart . . . Adventurer.'

The three set off together through the woods, moving as quietly as shadows. Tom and Jollity had their arms across each other's shoulders.

'Not long to your birthday, Tom,' said Cicero. 'You'll be thirteen soon, and it looks to me like the first snow will be a day or two early this year.'

Tom looked up at the stars. He thought he could make out a pattern in one of the constellations, peeping through the clouds. It looked like a strong standing figure aiming a bow and arrow.

Perhaps, Tom thought, they might be the Trueheart stars after all.

The three were soon swallowed up from view by the fading light. As they vanished among the trees the first flakes of snow began their slow dance downwards and the forest trees of the Land of Stories were left to themselves; they would soon be shivering a little in their white winter wear.

THE END